HE BRINGS OUT THE HOOD IN ME 4

NIKKI BROWN

FOLLOW ME ON SOCIAL MEDIA

Follow me on social media
Facebook: Author Nikki Brown
Facebook Reading Group: Nikki's Haven 🤍
Instagram: @nikkibrown_theauthor
Twitter: @NikkiBrownSWP
www.nikkibrownwrites.com

Text Nikki to 66866 to join my mailing list

ALSO BY NIKKI BROWN

CHAPTER ONE

*E*verything

Riding down the long dark road to the farm house gave Mega a little time to reflect on his life. He had been blessed to say the least. To have run a successful drug business and pave the way for his sons to be able to open legit businesses was unheard of where they were from. To say he was proud was putting it lightly.

Then his mind switched to his wife, their relationship had been so strained since Ziva came into their lives. Intimacy and communication was the foundation of their union, and it was now the two things that they were struggling with. Mega hoped that tonight all of that would change, he just wanted his family back.

"What the fuck?" Mega said as he pulled into the driveway of his home. Smoke was surrounding the front door of the house. Fear penetrated his heart the minute his eyes landed on Siya's car. *Something's not right.* Picking up the phone, he immediately dialed 911, quickly told them what was going on, and gave them an address.

Jumping out of the car with his phone in his hand, he ran to the front door. When he grabbed the knob, it was so hot that he had to draw his hand back. The pain never registered because his adrenaline was so high, he needed to find a way in that house and fast.

"Sir is everything okay?" He could hear the dispatcher, who he forgot he was talking to, yell through the phone. His mind was one figuring out a way to get in the house.

"Just get here, my wife is in the house. I can't get in the front door!" he yelled frantically.

"Sir just wait for help, they're in route."

"Fuck that!" He threw his phone on the ground and leaped off of the porch. The minute his feet hit the ground, he heard something from the distance. Praying that it was Siya getting out of the house, he took off to the back. A feminine silhouette took off towards the woods. The person was too tall to be his wife, but he knew who the figure belonged to. Mega bit down on his back teeth as tears rolled down his eyes! Guilt riddled his heart at the thought that she had done something to Siya. *I should have been here!* He thought as rage burned within him. He wanted Ziva dead and bad and if it was the last thing he did he would grant his wish.

"HEY!" he yelled and started towards them but the sound of the fire alarms going crazy stopped him and he turned towards the house. His heart was beating to the beat of his fear at the thought of Siya being hurt. He couldn't lose his everything, Siya was his everything.

Bursting through the back door, the smoke hit him in the face instantly bringing about a fit of coughing. Lifting the collar of his shirt across his nose, he made his way through the house. *Crash!* Something falling to the ground caused him to increase his speed in the direction of the sound. When he got to the living room his body froze and dread slowly slithered through him. Knots formed in his stomach as he took in the seen before him. The memories, the precious memories but right now the only thing that mattered was his wife.

"Siya! Baby!" his voice cracked as he called out for her. He tried his best to keep his mouth covered so that he wouldn't take in anymore smoke than he already had. "Oh shit!" He yelled out when he noticed her sprawled out on the floor surrounded by flames. "No baby."

With a sinking heart, he tried his best to think of a way to get to her. She was in the center of a ring of fire and it was closing in by the second. He knew that his window for saving her was dwindling so he did what he knew he had to do.

"Arggghhhh!" he yelled as he rushed through the standing flames. Unable to miss them, he felt the burning sensation through the black slacks that he wore. "Oh fuck!" *Crash!* Mega jumped back as a bookcase that was nearby fell over and on top of Siya's arm.

"Ahhhh!" Siya was in and out of consciousness due to the pain that her body was in, and the smoke that she inhaled made it difficult to hold her eyes open, but the minute she felt something fall on her arm, her eyes popped open. She flew into a fit of coughing mixed with moans of agony. "Help ME!" she screamed and then coughed some more.

Hearing the distress in her voice put some urgency in Mega's actions. "Ugggghhhhh!" He yelled out as he grabbed the bottom of the bookcase that was now engulfed in flames and tossed it off of her. He could smell his flesh as his fingertips burned from touching the open flames but none of that mattered to him, only Siya.

Once she was free of the debris, he lifted her and ran through the fire that was closing in on them. She moaned in between coughs as he made his way through the fire. He took off down the hall that he had just came from. His visibility was very limited, the thickness of the smoke made it hard for him to see where he was going but he wasn't gonna stop. Not until the both of them were safe.

A loud crash caused him to jump as he finally made it to the back door, he cringed at the sound. He held Siya close and pushed through the back door. Their house was destroyed, everything they worked for was gone and that hurt him, but not as much as the possibility of losing his everything.

"Baby! Baby!" He laid her down on the ground, she screamed out in pain.

Mega bit down on his bottom lip so hard that he drew blood. His heart hurt for her and he couldn't help but feel as if this was his fault. He was kicking himself for not just coming with her when she left. Leaning down placing his forehead on hers, he wanted to absorb everything that she was feeling. He wanted to take all of that pain away from her. He couldn't lose her. He didn't think that he could make it in life without Siya. "Hold on baby, please just hold on." His tears drifted down his face and settled at the collar of his shirt. "I need you baby, you gotta hold on."

Siya's eyes fluttered back in her head, her breathing had become shallow. Mega took a minute to take a look at her. His bones in his body shivered with rage as he noticed the blood coming from her head. He looked down at the arm of his shirt and it was saturated with her blood.

"No! No! No! open your eyes baby, you got to look at me." Mega deep voice roared in anguish. You could hear the pain that he felt dancing along the octaves of his baritone. Sniffing back tears he moved the hair that was in her face out of the way. She had a bruise on her jaw, and it looked as if her arm was broken. She had a really bad burn on her forearm, he hated himself right now for the position he put her in. There was no doubt in his mind that this was his fault. "Come on baby, I know it's hard but look at me."

His eyes traveled in the direction of where he saw Ziva run to. He could feel anger bellow in the pit of his stomach. There wasn't a hell hot enough for where he planned to send Ziva. She was going to hate the day that she ever laid eyes on anyone with the last name Maler and he put that on his kids.

Right when Mega got tired of waiting on someone to get there to help them, emergency personnel flooded the yard. As soon as they saw the condition of Siya, they administered oxygen and loaded her up in the ambulance. One of the EMTs tried to look at Mega's hands but he wouldn't let them. He told them when he knew that his wife was good, then and only then would he worry about himself. They tried to warn him about infection, but he wasn't trying to hear it.

Once they got to the hospital, she was wheeled back, and he was forced to sit in the waiting room. A nurse came out and talked him into letting her at least dress his fingers and cover them. Reluctantly, he allowed her to, but he refused to move from where he was.

After the nurse had him wrapped up, he sat back in the chair and closed his eyes. The sight of Siya laying in the middle of that ring of fire rushed his mind and the tears that flowed from his eyes were for his wife. He released every tear that he could because when the last one fell; nothing would surround him but death until Ziva took her last breath.

"Wah gwan? ("What's up?")" his thick accent resonated through the hospital waiting room pulling Mega out of his thoughts. Every syllable that left his lips raised Mega's pressure that much more. Whipping his head around, he came face to face with Marlin, Ziva's stepfather and the family connect.

When Mega's eyes met his, all he saw was red. He rushed him and threw him up against the wall of the waiting room and placed his forearm against his neck. *Click! Click! Click!* Mega turned his head slightly to see three guns pointed at him but he didn't care.

"Why the fuck are you here Marlin?" Mega said through clenched teeth. "Where the fuck is Ziva!"

"Mi come to check pan yuh (I came to check on you.)" Marlin barely got out because Mega's arm was pressed against his voice box. "Mi tap by di yaad an see all di babylon mi kno sup'm wrong, mi make sum calls and come here. (I stopped by the house and saw all the police; I knew something was wrong, so I made a few calls and came here." Marlins frail frame was no match for Mega's thick one, as much as he wiggled to get free, he just couldn't. "Mi cum inna peace mi bredda (I come in peace my brother.)"

"Back up before mi blow yuh brains out! (Back up before I blow your brains out!)" The gunman that was closest to Mega leaned in and said to him. Mega cocked back and elbowed the dude with so much force, it sent him flying back; and just as quickly returned his forearm back to Marlins neck with just as much pressure as before.

"Put the guns down." Marlin pointed at his guys, they hesitated but eventually put them down. The one that Mega knocked out had a mug on his face, and it was something about his eyes that Mega didn't like. The one thing that made his family successful was the fact that they fed off of people's vibes, and dude was giving a bad one. "Messa, put di gun down now!" Marlin yelled in his thick accent. *Messa. Noted.* Mega thought. "Move yuh bumbaclot arm mi a come here to warn yuh. (Move your muthafucking arm, I came here to warn you.)"

Mega looked around at where he was and slowly released

Marlin, he had never crossed Mega before and he didn't think he had now. He believed him when he said that he was there to warn him because their loyalty ran deep. His emotions were running high because of his wife and in his mind Ziva was Marlin's responsibility, that was the deal. Mega wanted to kill her all those years ago but Marlin assured him that she wouldn't be a problem, yet here they were.

Taking a few steps back Mega's chest rose and fell, his chest became tight and vision became a little blurry. He hit his chest a few times before he focused back on Marlin.

"My wife is in there, fighting for her life because that *bitch* tried to set her on fire." He pointed at the door where they wheeled Siya back. "If I hadn't of been rushing to get to her tonight, she would be dead."

The white of Mega's eyes turned bright red and his pupils took on the darkest shade of brown possible. If you were walking by and saw his face you would think that he was something out of a paranormal movie, he looked that crazy. Every vein that was visible was out and thumping to the beat of his racing heart.

"Mi looking fi har too (I'm looking for her too.)" Marlin tapped his chest.

"What the fuck do you mean? She was your responsibility. Why is she here?" Mega closed the gap that was in between them and the guys that were with Marlin closed theirs and Mega turned to face them. He didn't see fear in any of them except the one that Marlin referred to as Messa. "I'm gonna kill her!" He watched the men and again the only one that nonverbally responded was Messa. When his eyes moved to Marlin, his were void of any emotion.

"Nuh eff mi a get har fos. (Not if I get her first.)" Marlin's tone was so dark and demented that it caught Mega's attention. He listened as Marlin ran down everything that happened back home. He knew right then that shit was about to get real.

CHAPTER TWO

*W*here is she?

"The gi—girl walked in the house. She said that she was your friend and that y'all worked together," Amber sniffed. She was so distraught that she could barely form the words that she needed to tell them what happened. "I told her you weren't home and wh—when I went to shut the door, the man pushed it and made me fall."

"Where was Isis?" AD seethed. He prayed that they didn't do any of this in front of the baby. That would kill him if she had to see anything like that ever again. She was already scarred from the shit that her bitch ass daddy did to her mom. If she saw any of this, he promised that he would make him pay for it even more than he already would.

"She was right there on the couch." AD's fist tightened. "He slapped me and pushed me down and walked over to her.

I could see the fear in her eyes, she was so scared. I jumped on his back and tried to fight him, but he was too strong. Then that bitch pulled me by my hair to the ground and the two of them kicked and hit me while Isis balled up in a corner. Sh—she-" Amber burst out crying, she sobbed uncontrollably.

AD felt bad from what she had went through, but in his mind, the only thing that mattered was the fact that Isis was missing, and he needed to get her back. He wouldn't stop until he did. He leaned down to kiss Icelynn and then headed for the door. She grabbed his arm.

"No! You are not leaving me. I'm going, I don't give a fuck what you say." She pulled him back and walked towards the door.

"Should I call the police?" Amber said in tears.

"NO!" AD and Icelynn said in unison.

"I'll call a friend of mine from the police station over here and just tell him exactly what you told me. He will tell you what to do." AD gave her a warning look.

Amber didn't know what to do, she had never been in a situation like this before. She babysat to put herself through school. Most people's kids she watched were from the projects like she was, but she was excited when she was referred to Icelynn. Their house was always clean. Isis was a little firecracker but overall, she was a really good girl. This was by far the easiest gig that she had but she didn't know if she would be returning.

The gentleman that Icelynn was with right now scared her

for some reason so even if she wanted to run straight to the police station. Something was telling her not to, especially if he had friends there.

"Wh—what if—if they come back." She stammered.

"They won't, Officer Barret is on his way." AD said tone void of any emotions. He was trying his hardest not to spaz on the girl, but she was irritating him with all these questions. Icelynn could sense it.

"Just please Amber." She turned and left out the door. She shot Magic a text asking if she's seen Dimples and she text back immediately and said that she was there cleaning out her locker. Icelynn told her to keep her there until she got there. "Bitch was dumb enough to go to the job." Icelynn's veins quickly filled with hate and the only thing on her mind was hurting Dimples and Salem. "Take me to Onyx!" She demanded the minute they slid into his car. AD got on his phone and made a few calls for Spiff and Vinny to meet him at the club. Spiff said he was already there, and Vinny said he was babysitting, to give him a minute.

Icelynn sat in the passenger seat with her lips tucked in her mouth trying her best to hold in her sobs. The more she thought about the fact that he had her daughter, the harder it became to hold it in.

"Oh God, he has my baby!" she cried out scaring AD causing him to swerve. When he got control of the wheel again, he grabbed her thigh. Glancing back and forth between her and the road, his heart broke for her.

He loved Isis and he knew how she felt, that was her

daughter. She carried her for nine months, nurtured her for seven years for her to be snatched by the same monster she saved her from. That would mess with the strongest person.

"We're getting her back tonight," AD said with so much conviction. "Ion give a fuck if I have to tear this fucking city up. Isis will be home with us." Icelynn couldn't explain it but she believed him. She believed everything that he was saying, and she was grateful. She was grateful that he had come into their lives when he did. She didn't think she could have gone through this alone.

"He's evil," she said below a whisper. "He doesn't care about Isis; he will hurt her. You don't know the things he's done." She folded over in the seat and released a gut-wrenching scream.

Her scream pierced through AD's ears and straight through is heart. He really didn't know how much more he could take as a man, but he knew that now wasn't the time to crumble. Pain and turmoil seemed to be a revolving door in this life and his strength to push through it was incomparable.

"Icelynn, did you hear what I said?" He looked over at her and rubbed the back of her neck causing her shoulders to shiver.

"Oh God, he's gonna hurt my baby!" She cried even harder.

"ICE!" he yelled making her look up. "Did you hear what I said? She's coming home tonight." Icelynn nodded because she truly did believe him, but she couldn't help thinking about what Salem could be doing to her daughter, their daughter. "Do you believe me Ice?"

"Yes baby, I believe you. I trust you with everything in me," she revealed her truth.

"I need to ask you something, and I don't want you to get mad. Aight?" He glanced at her and the look in her eyes let him know that she knew exactly what he wanted to know. Nodding her head slowly, she looked straight ahead and prepared for his question. "What did he mean when he said that you had something that belonged to him? I didn't feel like he was talking about Isis, was he?"

"No! After he did what he did to me, I turned him in, and he got arrested. I was the only one that knew where his money was, and I cleaned his safe. We needed money to get away so that's what I did." She prayed that AD didn't think differently of her after her revelation. When he squeezed her thigh, she stared into his eyes and he gave her the reassurance she needed.

"When he got out, he sent word with some family that he was looking for me and he wanted his money. So I started getting money together from work. I almost had enough to pay him back. I just want him out of my life."

"That you won't have to worry about anymore. That nigga won't be in anyone's life anymore," AD's tone was cold and calculated.

"I just want my baby." She wiped her eyes with the back of her hands.

"I want her home too," AD said as he whipped into the parking lot of Onyx.

Before he could park, Icelynn was out of the car and headed inside. She had taken a few weeks off to prepare for her graduation that was a couple weeks away. She bypassed security and headed straight back to the locker room. She could hear arguing going on, but she wasn't interested in any of that; all she wanted was to get her hands-on Dimples to find out where her daughter was.

"If you don't move out my fucking way Magic, I got shit to do," Dimples' voice carried through the door way.

"I'm just trying to figure out why you taking shit out of other people's locker. Why you going through our shit, if you leaving then do that but don't touch our shit!" Magic protested. She didn't see Dimples stealing anything, but Icelynn was her girl so she did as she was asked.

"Bitch, I don't want nothing that you got but if your fat ass don't move from in front of this door, I'ma beat ya ass." That made Magic laugh but before she could say anything else Icelynn pushed through the door.

The look on her face, was enough to make Dimples try and push her way out the door but the minute she was in reach of Icelynn, she was being pulled in her direction. Icelynn grabbed her by the hair and slung her back against the table and joined her with a fist to the face.

"Where the fuck is my daughter bitch?" She hit her again, and again. "Where...is...my.... Fucking daughter!" Icelynn didn't even remember falling to the floor but there she was on top of Dimples hitting her repeatedly in the face. Grabbing her by her hair, she pulled her to her face. "Where is she?"

"I don't know."

"Bullshit." Icelynn cocked back and hit her dead in the mouth. Blood spewed from her mouth, the sight of it excited Icelynn. She had never really been a violent person, despite what she's been through, but when it came to her child, she became a different person and if she had to take a life, she told herself that she would. "Where is she?" she screamed down in Dimples' face.

AD walked over and pulled Icelynn off. She fought against his hold; she was pissed. The anger that she felt was unmeasurable and nothing could satisfy her but her daughter back in her arms.

"Chill baby," AD said in her ear. She was still swinging and trying to get away from AD but the minute his warm breath hit her skin, she calmed instantly. Looking him in the eyes with a tear stained face. "It's okay." He touched her lips with his.

AD was burning up on the inside, he wanted to be irrational. It would make him feel so much better to place his nine at Dimples' head and blow it clear off. He could get away with it because of where they were but he also knew that it would interfere with them getting Isis back.

"Please!" Dimples begged. "I didn't know he was going to do that. He told me to give him information about you and he paid me. Little stuff like your address and—"

"Bitch you told him where I lived?" Icelynn jumped at her.

AD had to catch her in mid-air and pull her back. He never realized how strong she was nor how mad she could get. He had to admit that it was turning him on.

"Get the fuck up, bitch!" He snatched Dimples up by her hair, she screamed out in pain drawing a little crowd. He brought her face to his and stared into her eye, Icelynn had the other eye swollen so she could only see out of one. "You know how I get down," AD said through gritted teeth. His patience and the whole trying to be calm thing was slowly going out the window. He was trying to control himself but that was one thing he wasn't good at.

"Please baby!" Dimples cried. She should have never brought her ass here but a few of the girls owed her money and she knew that she would need it to get out of town. Salem was waiting for her at her apartment, and they were heading to Chicago the minute she got back. She was kicking herself for not having him come with her.

"Bitch!" Hearing her call AD baby infuriated Icelynn and she tried to get at her again, but she felt someone else holding her. "Get your fucking hands off me." She turned around and saw a medium brown skinned dude that she remembers being at the farm house the day they had the cookout.

"AD nigga you good? Want me to clear the room." AD never took his eyes off of Dimples.

"Yeah nigga but get ya hands off my shorty." He threw over his shoulder and Icelynn snatched away from him. "Get everybody out of here."

Spiff pulled his gun out and started moving the strippers

and party goers that had made their way to the back. The owner gave Spiff a look and he shrugged his shoulders and told him to get the fuck out. Everyone cleared the room except for Magic who gave him a hard time but eventually left.

"Where is he?" Icelynn said now in tears. Her emotions were all over the place. She was bouncing in between furious and distraught, then they both mixed together and brought on a tinge of rage. She just wanted her daughter.

"Fuck this!" AD took the safety off his gun and put it in her mouth. Her eyes stretched as big as saucers. She shook her head and tried to move back. Tears filled her cheeks as she began to sob. "Oh, you ready to talk?" she nodded. AD slid the gun out of her mouth and waited for her to speak.

"They're at my apartment."

"Bitch!" Icelynn broke past AD and proceeded to beat the hell out of Dimples. She released every fear, every tear she dropped and every time her heart dropped at the thought of her not seeing Isis again or what he was doing to her.

"Baby!" AD pulled her off for a final time. "I need you to have a level head. We need her to get Isis back." That was the only reason that AD was as calm as he was, if you could even call what he was calm, but he knew that he could be ten times worse if the situation were different. "Let's go!" He picked Dimples up by the shirt and drug her out the door with Spiff and Icelynn in tow.

〜

"Shut the fuck up!" Salem voiced as Isis sat in the corner whimpering. She was nursing a busted lip that Salem gave her for crying out for her mother and AD. "You better be glad you ain't but seven, otherwise I'd have your ass out on the stroll." He chuckled evilly at his own joke.

"AD I need you." She wrapped her hands around her knees and squeezed them tightly. She softly rocked back and forth as she thought about the man that inserted himself into her and her mother's lives for the better. "Please save me." She laid her head on her lap.

"You can pray all you want. By the time God hears you, we'll be across the state lines on the way to Chicago." Again, he laughed making Isis cry a little louder than she originally was. She didn't want to leave her mom and AD, and she especially didn't want to be anywhere near her father.

"I hate you!" Isis yelled and Salem slapped her across the face with his hand. "I hope AD kills you!" she cried. She didn't understand the words that were coming out of her mouth, she just knew that she wanted this man that was in her space gone. She prayed that they never had to see him again. The things she watched him do to her mother were sick and she hated that she still had nightmares about it.

"You little bitch, I've turned bitches younger than you before. Keep talking and I'll be getting you ready for the track."

Salem was a monster; he didn't know anything about the word love. He had never felt it from anyone and the closest thing that he had to experiencing it was with Icelynn until she got pregnant with Isis. He told her to get rid of it and when she didn't, he became resentful. He didn't want kids because he knew that he was too selfish to care for them.

He wanted to live life with Icelynn and his hoes, but she didn't understand that. When she left and went to stay with her mom, he was hurt that she chose the baby in her stomach over what he was trying to build with her. He took it as a betrayal.

Finessing her heart and selling her dreams got him where he needed to be in his life and then he began to destroy hers. The only reason that he didn't put her on the track was because she was a virgin when he met her, and she was his favorite pussy to slide into. So he was selfish when it came to her.

The only time he let another man touch her was when she came in between his money. Candi was one of his best hoes and Icelynn messed her face up and she wasn't able to go and make any money. He had her lined up for a party that was guaranteed to bring in at least ten g's. When he sent the other girls, they canceled the party because Candi wasn't there.

So, Salem did what he had to do and since she loved Isis more than she loved him he made her watch. He didn't care about Isis, the only reason she was breathing was because of Icelynn. He knew that would be the only way to get her back to Chicago.

"Please God just let AD come and get me!" she cried to herself.

Tired of hearing her say AD's name, Salem walked over and jacked her up by her night gown causing it to rise above her *Shopkins* underwear. He threw her on the bed and looked down at her. Kids weren't his preference; teenage girls were but he had had his share of prepubescent girls. He didn't care if this was his daughter or not, pussy was all cut the same.

He pushed her gown up and Isis began to kick and swing with all her little might. One of her little feet caught him in the balls and he bent over. The kick was only strong enough to stun him for a second but not enough to stop him. She tried her best to get across the bed so she could run, but he caught her leg right as she was almost at the end.

"AHHHHHH!" she screamed and began to kick as hard as she could just like her mother taught her. Connecting with his nose causing blood to immediately drop from it and his eyes to water giving her the chance to wiggle out of his grip.

"Fuck! You little bitch!" he growled as she jumped off the bed.

Isis took off running towards the door and she ran right into something solid, screaming she shut her eyes and balled up on the floor. The sight alone had AD ready to murder Salem.

Scooping Isis up, he put her on his shoulder, as if you would a baby. Once she felt his arm wrapped around her, she knew that the stranger was none other than her AD. Her little body shook in his hold and every whimper drove AD more and more over the edge.

"It's okay baby girl," he said as he held her with one hand

and pointed his gun in Salem's direction. "I dare you to move," AD's tone was calm, he didn't want to frighten Isis any more than she already was.

"Damn I guess the bitch wasn't as solid as I thought." Salem laughed tucking his hands in his pocket. His eyes scanned the room trying to figure out a way to get out of this situation, but his chances were looking very slim right now.

"Baby girl, you trust me?" Isis whimpered and nodded her head that was buried in the crook of AD's neck. "Okay I need you to go outside with mommy and I'll be out in a minute."

"Nooo! AD, no please." She began to shake like a little leaf and that angered him. He leaned down a little to lower her to the ground, but she tightened her grip on his neck.

"Baby girl I need you to trust me." AD rubbed her back to reassure her.

Salem took this as a chance to try and get away. The minute he turned to jet back in the room where his gun was, AD fired a shot that tore through his shoulder.

"AHHHH!" Isis screamed and finally jumped out of his arms and ran to the door. AD walked to where Salem was and took his boot and shoved it in the wound that he had just created.

"Shit!" Salem hissed as he tried to move AD's foot with his free hand. "Fuck you and that little bitch. You better be glad you walked in when you did because I was gonna sample that pretty little pussy." He laughed and AD blacked out.

A sharp pain tore through his heart as he thought of Isis going through the shit that he had went through when he was younger. It was like he couldn't breathe as he hit Salem over and over again, his chest got so tight that he had to pause and grab it.

He felt like he was having a panic attack, but that didn't stop him from the damage that he planned to do to him.

"Fucking pervert, she's just a fucking kid!" he yelled out as the butt of his gun connected with Salem's eye. The sound of the bones in his face cracking with every hit satisfied AD to an extent.

"AD nigga we gotta go, blast that fool and come on!" Spiff said out of breath. He had just got a call from Cassidy looking for AD letting him know that their mother was in the hospital's burn unit. "It's ya moms, she's in the hospital man and it don't look good."

AD stopped mid swing, Salem was barely hanging on but hearing that Siya was in the hospital settled his rage and brought on a bout of fear. His energy quickly shifted as he turned towards his friend.

"Nigga you hear what the fuck I said?" Spiff glared at AD who was standing there looking at him with a shocked expression. He didn't have time for his boy to freeze, he needed to get to his family. "I got this, you get to the hospital and call me when you find out what's going on."

"Nah take him to the farmhouse."

"No can do, it's police and firetrucks everywhere. Someone set the house on fire with your mother in it. That's about all I know nigga."

"Uggghhhhh!" Salem began to wither around on the floor

in pain. AD's teeth gritted as he turned to go back to him. Every time he heard his voice, even if it was a moan, he thought about the way Isis was shivering in his arms.

"Nigga fuck that, yo family needs you. You can handle that shit later. I'll get him and her to my warehouse. Clean-up is outside waiting; I'll tell that nigga that it's been a change of plans. Might have to throw him a few more dollars but it is what it is," Spiff said sending a message to the crew that was outside. "Adoreé get the fuck out and go!" Spiff pointed to the door and AD turned and rushed out the door and into the car.

Icelynn was in the backseat with Isis, she was crying so hard that tears pulled in the rim of AD's eyes. His heart broke for her because he knew what something like that does to a kid. He didn't know if he did anything to her, but he knew that he could have possibly came close and even that could damage a child.

"He'll never hurt you again." AD looked in the rearview mirror and right into the eyes of Isis who was happy that the one man that she knew she could count on, saved her from the monster that helped create her. She nodded her head because she believed him.

AD's eyes shifted to Icelynn's whose were filled with tears. She mouthed the words thank you and he nodded his head. He didn't need a thank you, all he needed was for them to be safe and in his arms.

The look in his eyes worried Icelynn, it was like he was trying to tell her something without saying it out loud. She really didn't put anything past Salem, so she leaned down and kissed the hand print mark on her cheek and got choked up all over again.

"Isis I need to ask you something, and I need you to tell me the truth. Even if it's hard to say. Okay baby?" Isis sniffed back the tears that were falling speedily.

"Okay mommy." The innocence in her voice made AD tighten his grip on the steering wheel, he didn't know if he could take the answer that was about to come out of her mouth. If she said anything other than no then he didn't know what he would do.

"Did Salem touch you?" Her question was vague, and Isis didn't know how to answer it. He touched her when he slapped her across the face and threw her on the bed but that was it. She didn't want to lie to her mom, but she didn't want to make it seem like he did anything else to her. So she thought about the words that she wanted to say.

"He hit me in the face and grabbed me by my night gown and threw me on the bed." She swallowed hard; AD's heart fell to his stomach as he dreaded what else was about to come out of her mouth. "He said that he was gonna steal me and take me to Chicago and put me on a track." She looked up in her mother's eyes. "What's a track?"

"Nothing that you will ever have to worry about." She grabbed her daughter and squeezed for what felt like the hundredth time. They were safe and she had AD to thank for that. "Did you call and see what was going on with Siya? I heard Spiff on the phone, and he sounded like it was urgent."

For a brief moment AD's mind had blocked out what Spiff told him. He was too focused on making sure that Isis was okay. He patted his pocket to grab his phone and he realized that it was off.

"My phone is dead. Fuck!"

"What's wrong with Mawmaw?" Isis perked up; she had grown close to Siya in the short time they had known each other. She's only had one grandma and that was grandma Isabell. When she met Siya, she instantly took to her. Isis would be sad if something were to happen to her.

"I'm sure it's gonna be okay baby," Icelynn's voice was soothing and even though she was talking to Isis, he needed to hear that too.

CHAPTER THREE

*B*reaking Point

    "How in the fuck this bitch keep getting close to my mother?" Cassidy seethed after hearing what the doctor said. He couldn't contain his anger. First at the restaurant and now Siya lay in the hospital fighting for her life.

Cassidy's masculine arms were across his chest as he looked out into the waiting area at no one in particular. Key's eyes were burning a hole through him, but he paid her no mind. He tried to give her his keys to go home but she refused to leave him, so that was on her. Right now his only focus was Siya Maler and figuring out how to get his hands on the person responsible for this.

"She was raised by a kingpin. Much like you, she knows her way around the game." Mega lifted his head out of his hands. "Hell, I taught her some of what she knows when I was with the bitch." Venom dripped from every word. "The one thing that I didn't teach her...was to not fuck with me," he said through clenched teeth.

"I got people looking for her, the only way she'll be able to get out of the state of North Carolina is on foot." Kahleno stared straight ahead. He didn't know how much more his family could take; as bad as he wanted to fold, he couldn't, and he wouldn't. The city was about to feel their pain, until Ziva was caught.

Sutton rubbed his back as she tried to keep her tears at bay. The pregnancy already had her emotional, but she knew that Kahleno didn't need that from her right now.

Kahleno stared down into Sutton's eyes, he could see that she was just as hurt because Siya had become like a surrogate mother for her since they had been dealing with each other. She loved her and vice versa.

"She has to be okay." Sutton's lips trembled as he pulled her into him.

Cassidy couldn't take it anymore, seeing Sutton breakdown was too much for him. He needed to get away, so he turned to walk to the bathroom. He needed to hear something about his mother before he exploded. Every time the doors opened to the back panic unfurled in his chest.

When he got into the bathroom, he slammed the door and threw his back against it. Cassidy was at his breaking point, he was tired of people fucking with his family, all of them were. Cassidy felt like he needed a minute away from everybody because he could feel his anger building up and he didn't want to spaz even though them not telling him anything about his mother granted him the right to.

He heard a knock at the door, he didn't say anything because right now he needed to be alone so that he could get his emotions in order before he ended up behind bars for being irrational.

"Cas?" Key's sweet voice bounced off the wall of the bathroom.

They had been getting to know each other and he had to admit that she was someone that he could see himself with long term. He still felt like she was a bit of a mystery to him, and he needed to find out more about her, but from what he knew they matched well.

"I'll be out in a minute." She could hear the pain painting his voice and it didn't sit well with her. She was used to the smart mouth Cassidy who said whatever and did whatever came to mind. This softer side of him, this emotional side drew her to him even more.

Not taking heed to his request to be alone, she slipped in the bathroom with him. When she was near him, she reached out to touch him, but he moved from her grasp. Cassidy was the true definition of an Alpha male and any ounce of emotion was considered weakness when it came to him. He couldn't speak for other men, but he wasn't built for emotions.

"You want to talk about it?" Key chose her words wisely. She didn't want to push but she also knew that even though he requested it, he didn't need to be alone.

"Last time I checked; you went to school for hair not psychology. So get the fuck out of here with that bullshit, Key." He threw out there refusing to look at her. She had the kind of eyes that would draw you in and have you doing all kinds of shit that you didn't want to do.

"But I'm a woman with feelings so I get it." She snaked her body so that she was now in his line of sight. He looked down at her and just like he thought, she was bringing out things that he didn't want to be out. He could feel the tears on the brinks, so he pushed past her, but she grabbed his arm. "You're a man that hides his feelings, but you don't have to Cassidy, not with me."

"You don't know nothing about me Key."

"I know that you're scared that if you show how you're feeling about your mom, that you'll feel less than a man. So you'd rather punch things and kick them over instead of letting someone be there for you."

Cassidy thought about what she was saying, and she was right. If he could take his aggression out on someone at this present moment, he would, and it would feel amazing. True enough he's cried before, but he hated it, it made him feel soft, so he was trying his best to keep all of that under control.

"What the fuck you want me to do Key? Did you hear what the fuck she did to her?" He pointed to the bathroom door. His voice echoed off the walls and traveled into the waiting room.

Kahleno stood to go and make sure that everything was

okay. If anyone knew his brother and how he was when he felt helpless it was him, but his father grabbed his arm and urged him to sit. He knew that Cassidy had a connection with Key and if they were going to work out then she needed to understand this side of him.

"I want you to let me be there for you," she said honestly. "Yell, scream, do whatever you have to do but don't push me away. I'm telling you, I'm right here Cassidy." She closed the gap that he had created between them. "Right here."

Pulling her into him, he enclosed her into his arms and lightly squeezed, it was like a feeling of relief bullied its way into his heart. Resting his chin on top of her head, he let one lone tear roll down his face because that's all that he would allow.

Everything else was reserved for the day he got his hands on that bitch Ziva, he couldn't wait to make that bitch pay for everything that she had done to his family.

Crashing his lips against hers, Cassidy allowed the kiss to linger as his apology for being so cold to her. Since they walked in, he wouldn't allow her to touch him and he stayed as far as he could away from her. If he could have dropped her off at home, he would have but the hospital was right down the street from where they ended up.

"Oh and I never said I went to school for psychology smart ass. You better be glad I wanted to be nice otherwise I would have cussed you out," she sassed and then kissed his lips again. He smirked for the first time since he got the call.

"You ain't gone do shit." He kissed her again feeling somewhat relieved.

"Whatever nigga, you straight?" she asked him, and he nodded his head, but she didn't believe him. "Umhmm well lets go back out here, she should be out of surgery soon."

After they all got there, their father told them what happened. They were all tore up about it. She was getting out of hand and they needed to get a grip on it all. Cassidy was pissed that AD wasn't here with them and had tried to call him multiple times, so when he walked out of the bathroom and he saw him walking up, he figured that he would tell him exactly how he felt.

"What happened? What the fuck is Spiff talking about?" AD said the minute he was in the waiting room surrounded by his family. His chest rose and fell with anticipation, he needed to know that she was okay.

"Where the fuck you been?" Cassidy boomed the minute he laid eyes on his youngest brother. "You didn't see us calling you? We got enough going on without having to worry about you and your bullshit." He got in AD's face and AD just stared at him with his fist balled by his side.

He had no intentions on going at it with his brother, but he wasn't about to be disrespected either. When he tried to walk past Cassidy, he stopped him by pushing him in the chest with his hand. AD stood back and then stepped in Cassidy's face.

Cassidy was thicker and taller than Ad, but that didn't move him, he would rock with the best of them and Cassidy knew that. With everything that had already happened that night, it would be in Cassidy's best interest to move.

"Touch me a-fucking-gain and I'ma forget we share the same fucking blood." AD's nose flared and the vein in the side of this neck stuck out. Icelynn walked up with Isis in tow and grabbed his hand. Isis went around to the other side with a tear stained face and grabbed his other hand.

That instantly calmed AD, he looked at Icelynn and then turned around to scoop Isis up in his arm. Luckily, she had clothes in his trunk from that night that her and Icelynn stayed with him, and she was able to put them on. He didn't want her walking around without clothes on and he didn't want to take them back to that house. Just the thought of leaving them alone right now wasn't on his list of things to do. They were gonna be by his side until Salem met his final resting place by his hands.

AD moved around Cassidy who noticed the blood spatters on his brother's shirt. AD didn't bother to change; he didn't care who saw him. All he wanted to do was make sure that his mother was okay so his heart could be at peace if only for a night.

"The fuck happened to her face?" Cassidy snapped out of the initial state of anger and noticed that Isis had a huge hand print on the side of her face. "AD I know you hear—"

"Yo, I'm trying real hard not to knock you the fuck out because I know shit with moms got you stressed, but you need to chill the fuck out on some real shit!" AD yelled causing Isis to jump in his arms and he narrowed his eyes at Cassidy.

"You right man, I'm fucked up right now." Cassidy shook his head. He knew that how he was acting wasn't him, but he was looking for someone to take what he was feeling out on. "For real though, what happened to baby girl's face?"

AD shook his head. "We'll talk about that later." He clenched his jaw just thinking about what Isis had been through tonight. "She's good now, what's up with ma? She good? Spiff said shit wasn't looking good."

Everyone looked around trying to find the right way to explain to him what went down without bringing up everything that he had just went through, but it was kind of hard. Cassidy slipped his hands in his pockets and leaned against the wall. Key walked over and wrapped her hand around his waist.

"Son..."

"Don't fucking pacify me, tell me what the fuck is up." Isis squeezed him tighter. She could feel that he was getting upset and she didn't like it. She took a deep breath and leaned over and kissed his cheek.

"Here let me take her, I want to take her down to get checked out anyway." Icelynn reached for Isis but she tightened her grip on AD's neck. "Come on baby, we'll be right back, but we need to get you checked out.

"Noooo!" Isis kicked and screamed while Icelynn was trying to pry her out of AD's arms. She felt safe when she was with him. She didn't want to let that feeling go and she knew if he was out of her presence, she wouldn't feel that anymore.

It broke Icelynn's heart just seeing that, she didn't try to hide the tears that fell from her face. She hated Salem and wouldn't be satisfied until she knew that he was dead and gone. Once she had Isis out of AD's arms, he was on his feet reaching for her again.

"Just wait and we'll go together, aight?" He wiped Icelynn's face with his free hand since Isis had climbed back in his other. AD sat down with her on his shoulder while she silently cried. "I told you he would never hurt you again, do you believe me Isis?" She didn't answer verbally she just nodded her head. AD slowly rocked her back and forth trying to calm her down, while Icelynn laid her head on his shoulder and closed her eyes to stop the headache that was brewing from crying.

Everyone looked on shocked, wondering what happened, but no one else asked. It was clear that now was not time for the conversation to take place, but they all made mental notes to ask about this once little Isis was out of ear shot.

"It was Ziva," Kahleno finally said halting AD's rocking and causing Icelynn's head to pop up.

AD's body became tense as he leaned up a little to make sure he heard his brother right. Were they saying that his mother was in the hospital because his biological mother put her there? How was he supposed to feel about this? Even though he didn't care for Ziva at all, but that meant that he was gonna have to kill her if his father or brothers didn't get to her first.

"Bruh..." was all that AD could say before the doors to the back swung open and the doctor came out, it was the same doctor that took care of Kahleno when he was shot. So he already knew what to expect from this family which was why the minute Siya was out of surgery she was moved to a private room at the end of the hall.

"Family of Siya Maler," he announced even though he already knew who they were. He would never forget the face of the man that put fear in his heart. When Mega stepped forward, the doctor swallowed hard. "She suffered a broken femur, dislocated shoulder and the shot to the back of the head gave her a concussion. She also has third degree burns on her right arm." His eyes traveled to each one of the men that stood before him. He could feel the rage radiating off of each of their bodies, causing him to take a step back to create some distance. "Her lab work shows that she has Carbon Monoxide poisoning from the smoke inhalation and—" AD cut him off.

"Will she be okay?"

"Depending on how much smoke she took in, it could cause some issues with her neurovascular system. But—"

"But what?" Cassidy stepped up this time invading the doctors space.

"HBO," the doctor said and every man standing in front of him eyebrows dented in and he knew that if he didn't speak soon that he was about to feel their wrath. "Hyperbaric Oxygenation."

"The fuck is that?" Cassidy asked ready to pounce on the doctor with all of this theatrical bullshit. He wanted to know what they needed to do to make their mother better and he was going in circles with the answers.

"It's a procedure where we will place Mrs. Maler in a chamber where she will have to stay in for twenty-four hours and we will administer continuous oxygen. Because of the amount of oxygen going into her body, she will need to be watched closely. It causes reduction in the symptoms of the nervous system and it will make her recovery time quicker."

"So she's gonna make it?" Kahleno stepped up and stood beside Cassidy. The doctor was suddenly starting to feel a little uncomfortable and claustrophobic with how close they were, but he understood them wanting answers, so he swallowed hard and took a step back.

"She took in a lot of smoke and she was burned pretty bad, on top of the beating that she took," the doctor inhaled roughly and shook his head. "I don't know how but she made it out of surgery. She's still in critical condition but I think with support and some therapy, she will be just fine." The doctor delivered a smile and put everyone at ease but Mega.

Nothing would put his heart at ease until he looked his wife in the face and kissed her lips. No one was there, they didn't see her going in and out of consciousness, they didn't witness the flames surround her, they didn't hear her cry out.

His heart ached at the memory, but until he could hear her voice, nothing would satisfy him.

"Can I see her?" Mega interrupted the doctor further explaining what they would have to do. The doctor nodded his head and offered up a small smile.

"Because I remembered your family, she has a private room. Same room as your son." The doctor nodded and Mega held his hand out for him to shake.

"Thank you... for everything." The doctor nodded and allowed all of them to make it up to her room.

A few hours went by, the doctor came in and told them that they would be to get her to have the Hyperbaric Oxygenation therapy soon. They told him that she had been moving around a little and wincing like she was in pain. He let them know that the pain medicine may be wearing off and if she seems to be in too much pain, call the nurse and they'll administer more medicine.

Isis was curled up at the end of the bed, she had grown to love Siya in the time that she had been around her. She looked at her as a second grandma, so seeing her like this hurt her feelings. With everything that her little heart had been through tonight she just wanted to give her a hug and hear her say, *"Life gives it's hardest battles to its toughest soldiers, are you tough Isis?"*

"I'm so glad you left when you did," Kahleno interrupted the silence of the room. Mega raised his head from his hands and looked towards his son.

"Me too son, me too." He shook his head. The guilt that

filed his heart was unrivaled to anything he's ever felt. Because of his actions, his wife was suffering, and he didn't know if he could live with that. "I'm sorry baby," he said as he laid his hand on top of Siya's.

"This ain't on you pops." Cassidy was in the corner with Key on his lap. He had tried to get her to go home but she didn't feel right not being here for him. Her heart wouldn't let her. She called and checked on Kane and Vinny said they were fine and to keep him up to date on what was going on.

Cassidy was happy that she decided to stay because he didn't know how much he needed someone through a time like this until the thought of her leaving pained him. He looked down at her and her eyes were on him, just like they've been since they had gotten to the hospital.

"Yeah don't do that, she gone be good. She too stubborn to die." Everyone laughed at AD's attempt to lighten the mood.

Siya stirred in her sleep. She could have sworn that she heard AD's voice, but the last thing she remembered was passing out in the living room floor. As the scene replayed in her mind, her eyes shot open and she tried to sit up.

"No baby, you gotta calm down. You're in the hospital." Mega grabbed her by the shoulders and tried his best to get her to look up at him. She was panicking and he didn't want her to go into distress. "Baby look at me." Her eyes scanned the room fanatically like she was looking for someone and when her eyes landed on AD, she reached for him with her good arm. She still winced in pain because that was the shoulder that the doctor had to put back in place.

"Adoreé," her voice was harsh and hoarse, almost like she had smoked four packs of cigarettes back to back. She continued to reach for him until he was in her presence. "Y—ou," she tried to swallow but no saliva would produce for her to do so, "my son! You are—"

"Shhhh, shhhh, shhhh, mama stop it." AD tried to quiet her as tears gathered in the corner of his eyes. He was about to break down thinking that his mother had been through everything that she had and all she was worried about was how he felt about the Ziva situation. "She means nothing to me and if I get to put the bullet in her head myself then it would make me the happiest man a-fucking-live." The passion in his tone made Siya's heart flutter but that's not what she wanted to tell him.

She shook her head back and forth quickly, "No! No! She stole—" she flew into a fit of coughing. The cough was so deep and harsh that it caused alarm with everyone in the room. Mega jumped up and opened the door to yell for the nurse who was already in a full fledge run because of the machines going off. The doctor wasn't far behind.

All three brothers stood back with tears in their eyes as they watched the nurse and doctor work on Siya. They all had the same thing running through their minds, and they couldn't wait to act on it.

CHAPTER FOUR

*C*onnected

Cassidy sat in the car in front of Key's house for what felt like forever, she was right by his side rubbing his thigh. He would glance at her every now and then but then focus back straight ahead at nothing in particular. She wanted to pick his brain on where his thoughts were, but she felt like he just needed to get lost in them and find his own way back out.

"Thank you," he simply said.

"For?" Key turned her body, so that she was facing him. She didn't need or want an apology from him, she was there for him because she wanted to be. He had come in her life and breathed a little life into her boring life, and she was grateful. Being there for him was the least she could do.

"You didn't have to stay; you could have left and for that

I'm thankful." He leaned his head back on the headrest and turned to look at her. His eyes explored the story that whirled around hers, she was a mystery to him. That both scared and intrigued him at the same time.

"Would you have left me?" Her eyes bounced around his as he pondered her question. "If that were me and it was my brother or my son, would you have left me?"

"Hell no, I ain't built like that."

"So you're insinuating that I am?" She raised her brows.

That was one of the things that drew Cassidy to Key, she was always challenging him. She had a way of making him see things through her point of view, even if he didn't want to. He couldn't figure out how she did, but he liked how she made him think about things.

"Did I say that, smart ass?" He smirked at her. She was trying her best to mug him but when the corners of her mouth turned up into a smile, she quickly turned away. "That's what yo ass get trying to be hard, soft as a damn crème puff."

"Yo, you can go to hell with that one." She laughed. "I love that you bring out the silly side of me. I thought I lost that all those years ago." She shook her head and sighed, not wanting to think about the past. "No but seriously, I like you Cassidy even though we've only been on half a date," she giggled, and he released a chuckle. "I feel connected to you for some reason and when you hurt I do too. I've only met your mother a couple of times when she's come to the shop, but she seems like good people and didn't deserve that."

Cassidy grinded his teeth thinking about what his mother was going through right now. It was like his family just couldn't catch a break, and it was driving them all crazy. They just wanted to be happy and now after meeting Key, he just wanted to run his farm and be happy, but life had other plans for him, and he didn't know why.

"I'm sorry for that too, I didn't know none of that shit was gone go down."

"Stop apologizing for shit you couldn't control. I've lived this life, so I know how it goes."

"Shut the hell up Key, you square as your fucking head." Cassidy laughed, and she mushed him in the head and giggled at his insult.

"Nigga, did you forget who my brother was? I been dealing with this lifestyle since before he could get a damn license." She shook her head and Cassidy nodded his. "You want to come in?"

Cassidy looked in his rearview mirror, he wanted to go in and hang with Key a little more, but he didn't want Jayla to try and start no shit. Even though she was there with Vinny, he also knew that she could be messy as hell when she wanted to be. He couldn't believe that she was still here after he told Vinny he fucked with her but that wasn't his concern. He was completely done with her now and had every intention on figuring out what was up with Key.

Key followed his eyes and smacked her lips. She turned to get out of the car, she didn't know why she felt so jealous all of a sudden when they weren't together but the thought of him caring about someone else's feelings pissed her off and she wasn't about to pretend like she wasn't.

"Chill man." Cassidy grabbed her arm and forced her to look at him. "You know I used to fuck with her, ain't shit no more because I'm trying to see what's up with you." He told her honestly. "I just want to make it clear that if she starts some shit, that you know how to curve it."

"I'm grown Cassidy, we good. Plus, my brother's mouth ain't something that she wants to deal with if she tries something stupid like coming for me on the strength of you." She smirked.

"None of that has anything to do with me, I just want to make sure that this ain't gone interfere with this." He motioned between the two of them. "I'm not in the right head space to be arguing with you over some shit that you already know." He gave her a warning look and she rolled her eyes.

"Get out of the car, I'll make you some breakfast." The sun had risen and set its bright self in the sky. They spent the entire night at the hospital and their dinner was ruined so neither of them had ate or slept.

Cassidy followed her out and went into the house. It was quiet, everyone seemed to be still sleep. He took a seat on the sofa at Key's request while she walked in the kitchen and began to prepare breakfast for everyone. Reaching for his phone, he had a missed call from Kahleno that he didn't notice so he decided to call him back.

"Sup bro," he said the minute Kahleno's tired voice came over the phone.

"Not shit, where you at?"

"Nigga you nosey, why you worried about where I'm at?" Cassidy said laying his head back on the couch. Tired was an understatement and he would do anything to just climb in the bed and close his eyes, preferable Akiya's bed but her son was home and he would never disrespect him like that.

"You at Key crib nigga," Kahleno chuckled and then said something to Sutton. "What time you going back to the hospital?"

"Well, we can't see her until she gets done with that therapy shit so when she come out of that, I'm going up there." Cassidy closed his eyes for a second but opened them when he felt someone in his space. When his eyes opened a grimace covered his face as he came face to face with Jayla.

"Yeah me too but I need to holla at you about some shit, it's real fucked up and we need to go to the farm house and meet the insurance people and check on our other shit," Kahleno said referring to the other barns in the back of the house.

"Oh fuck!" Cassidy said, the barn hadn't even crossed his mind. He knew for a fact if anything was wrong or missing at his farm that he was gone tear some shit up. "I didn't even think about that shit."

"Nah yo shit good, and AD's lab is straight. Connects at the station shot a text after they checked on everything for me." Kahleno said and then yawned. "I'll hit you up when I head over there. Have you talked to AD?"

"Nah," was all Cassidy said as Jayla stood in front of him with her arms crossed across her chest and a mug on her pretty face. She was acting as if she had any reason to be mad. "I'll hit you back when I leave here."

"Aight tell *sis* we appreciate her for being there for us." The sarcasm in his voice caused Cassidy to hang up the phone in his face.

Running his hands down his face, he wasn't in the mood to deal with Jayla and her shit. So he decided to ignore her. Closing his eyes, he leaned his back on the couch and crossed his arms across his chest. He figured he would get a few minutes of sleep while Key cooked and then he needed to get to the farm house.

Feeling the couch dip in beside him, he thought that she was sitting down so she could talk with her nagging voice; but when he felt her straddle him, his eyes popped open and he pushed her to the ground.

"The fuck yo stupid ass doing Jayla?" He stood up and brushed his pants down because he was sure that she didn't have anything under that robe she had on. "Nasty bitch, didn't you just lay up with my nigga and you sit yo dirty pussy on my lap? Fuck wrong with you." His eyebrows were dented in and his lip was turned up, he was truly disgusted.

If looks could kill, Jayla would be chopped up in a million pieces. All she wanted was for Cassidy to acknowledge her, the only reason that she was even here was because he refused to be with her the way she wanted him to be with her. She knew that he told her from the beginning that it would never be anything, but she thought that if she gave enough that he would meet her half way but it never happened.

When she met Vinny, she didn't know that he was connected to the Maler men but when she saw Cassidy's car at his house the night before, she could have crawled out of her skin right then and there and died. She couldn't get out of the car, and when she saw Vinny address her and then Cassidy, she knew that she was caught.

The envy that burned within her seeing him be affectionate with another woman had her mad as hell and even more determined to get with Vinny. What she didn't know was that Cassidy could care less and it made it that much easier for him to close the door completely on what little they did have.

"You really gone treat me like that?" She asked as if she was hurt by what was going on. Like she wasn't just sexing Vinny merely minutes ago.

"What the fuck is going on?" Key walked slowly in the living room with a bowl that she was mixing the pancakes up in. She looked from Cassidy, who seemed to be aggravated, to Jayla who looked on with envy in her eyes. "Cassidy."

"I already told you what was up." Was all he said as he laid his head back on the couch.

"Jayla, where yo funny looking ass go?" Vinny came through the house rubbing his eyes with nothing but a pair of ball shorts on. Jayla had just got through riding the hell out of his dick and was supposed to be heading to the bathroom to clean off, but she never returned.

After Cassidy told him that he fucked with her, he came in the house and shut the door. About twenty minutes later, he heard a knock on the door, and she walked in, dropped to her knees, pulled his shit out, and started sucking the hell out of his dick. He had almost forgot he was babysitting, thank goodness that Kane was in his room playing Fortnite.

The two of them spent the majority of the night in the room exploring and lusting over each other because that's all it was for either of them. When Vinny's eyes met Cassidy's, the both of them burst out laughing making Jayla feel as small as the amount of respect that either of them had for her.

"It wasn't funny about a little while ago when I was riding your dick and you were ignoring her calls. I take it she's *pretty girl,* right?" Jealousy dripped from every word she spoke, and she didn't care, she had already made a fool of herself so she may as well let it all out.

Key could feel her temperature rising, she was about to snap but she was trying her hardest not to. He told her in the car what could happen, so she really couldn't trip, but the fact that he didn't call her back because he was fucking another chick bothered her and it was hard to hide that.

"Yep, a little while ago we were just friends," he pointed back and forth between himself and Key. He could feel her staring a hole through him and he knew that he would have to answer to that but right now wasn't the time. "And just a while ago you was fucking my nigga." Cassidy shrugged.

"Whoa, the fuck going on?" Vinny looked at Jayla who was in the process of rolling her eyes at Cassidy. "Yo, you on some real hoe type shit my nigga. Get yo dumb ass in there and put ya clothes on and get the fuck out. Pussy was a little dank anyway. Get the fuck out of here." Vinny shook his head and then turned to Cassidy. "Nigga wasn't no disrespect; I just wanted some pussy. After you said you smashed, I had already called me another little thang-thang, but she burst through the door and swallowed my shit and I couldn't even think straight my nigga, you know how it is." Vinny pointed at Cassidy and he nodded his head and laughed at Vinny.

"Alright! Alright! That's enough." Key stepped in. She was starting to feel a little disrespected and she actually felt bad for Jayla. "That was disrespectful."

"Yeah tell me about it." Jayla said and then mumbled something else.

"My love, you need to give them something to respect, but for now you can get dressed and get the hell out." Key felt bad for her until she remembered what she walked in on. She was actually happy that Cassidy reacted the way that he did.

"The fuck yo goofy ass still sitting there for, get the fuck up." Vinny grilled Jayla as she got up and ran back to the room with him following close behind. "Yo you can suck my dick before you go though, for giving me a fucking headache." Vinny stopped mid-way and turned around, all this made him forget what was going on. "How's ya mom doing? Is she good? AD text me but he didn't really say much."

"I don't know man. They got her in some kind of Oxygen

therapy or some shit like that, that's supposed to help. I just needed to get out of that place for a hot minute. But we going back later," Cassidy said feeling slightly bad about leaving but there wasn't anything that they could do, and he knew Mega was there so that made him feel a little better.

"Let me know when y'all go up, I'm going too." Cassidy nodded. "I'm about to make this bitch swallow my shit again before I put her out." Vinny walked to the back where Jayla was and slammed the door. They argued for a minute and then everything went quiet.

"I swear something is wrong with him." Key shook her head and headed back in the kitchen. She was low key pissed about the revelation from Jayla, she didn't want to be around him at the moment. She needed a chance to calm down, but Cassidy couldn't give her that.

He smoothly walked his way into the kitchen and leaned against the door frame. He watched as she moved around the kitchen purposely trying to ignore him. At this point, he didn't mind because the way her thick ass filled out the leggings that she changed into made his dick hard.

The soft curls that framed her round face made her look innocent. Her pouty lips were a turn on in themselves, even though they were sticking out a mile long right now because she was mad. Taking a few steps to close the gap, he pressed his semi hard on against her ass. She froze against the sink and took a deep breath.

Leaning down his lips connected with her neck and he kissed it lightly causing her to shudder. He moved up a little and then kissed her again, and then again until she escaped his hold, but he grabbed her before she got too far.

Cassidy pulled her back to him and positioned her so that she was looking up at him. He leaned down and pressed his lips against hers. When his tongue invaded her mouth, she released a soft moan that had Cassidy's dick ready to burst through his pants.

"I'm mad at you," Key said when she regained possession of her lips again.

"I know that shit was fucked up but I ain't gone lie to you, a nigga fucked up." He shrugged like it was no big deal and Key smacked her lips. "I'm not saying it like it was nothing, I'm just saying that I wasn't thinking, I just wanted my dick wet."

"Well I'm not dealing with shit like that. I been through a lot and it taught me my worth. I like you but I'm not lowering my standards to be with you either. So if you want to fuck what you know then that's fine, we can be friends. If you trying to know me then that's what it's got to be *period*!"

All the shit that her ex put her through, she wouldn't dare enter into anything else and end up the same way. She promised herself that she would never hold anyone else's needs over her, and her son's and she meant it. She didn't care how fine he was.

"I know that shit and that's why I'm here." Cassidy said looking down at her light skin glowing under the kitchen lights. Her eyes searched his for any indication that what he was saying wasn't true, but she didn't find any. All she saw was everything that she ever wanted in a man, now she just prayed that he was everything that her heart thought he was. "I'm feeling the shit out of you Akiya, and you got my attention. All of it, you won't have to ever worry about a bitch coming to tell you anything about me and that's my word."

"I hear you, just so we're on the same page because a bitch all out of chances." She pointed at him and he smirked.

"Yo short ass don't scare nobody," he said against her lips that he had connected with once again.

Cassidy's hands wrapped around and pulled her closer to him and he deepened the kiss. Key snaked her arms around his neck and relished in the essence of him. She didn't expect to get as turned on as she did. When he grabbed her ass, she jumped up and wrapped her legs around his waist. He pulled away from her and looked down at her warning her to stop grinding against him before she started something that she wasn't prepared for.

"I want you so fucking bad right now," Key revealed, and it made Cassidy smile, he loved a woman that could express what she wanted and when she wanted it. Key was exactly what he wanted in a woman. She was driven, she had her own, and most of all, she wasn't gone take his shit.

Normally, Cassidy would take time and evaluate the situation before he started thinking about the future, but he felt so connected to her. Cassidy was picky in who he spent his time with, but she didn't even have to ask for his time, he wanted her to have it and that's how he knew this was something worth pursuing. It was like he couldn't stop himself from wanting her, and he was low key trying to find something wrong with her to make him take a step back but there was nothing there. Her vibe was infectious and had him throwing caution to the wind. He was invested, his feelings were invested, and he was moving forward with her beside him.

"You're fucking perfect, you know that." He attacked her lips again and she had to pull back.

"I'm not perfect, no one is. We've all had our shit, it's all about how you grow out of it." She looked deep into his eyes, she wanted him to hear her because her past wasn't a pretty one. She didn't want him putting her on a pedestal only to knock her down when he finds out she's not as *perfect* as he thought she was.

"But you're perfect for me." He kissed her again. Long and deep before he let her go and went back into the living room so she could finish cooking. When he sat down, he closed his eyes and smiled. Key was his person, his one.

~

Cassidy tried to turn over, but something was stopping him, he held his arms over his head and stretched only to be stopped again. His eyes fluttered open and he looked around not knowing where he was. Jumping up, his eyes scanned the room and that's when he realized that he was still at Key's house.

He had fallen asleep on the couch by the time that Key had finished cooking and he was sleeping so peaceful she didn't have the heart to wake him. So she helped him lay down and went to get her a few hours of sleep herself. Kane had left with Vinny to go shoot ball and she welcomed the break.

Getting up, Cassidy walked to the kitchen to see that she had fixed his plate and left it on the table. He smiled at the gesture and it made him even more sure of his choice to pursue things with her. Throwing the plate in the microwave, he made his way through the rest of the house in search of his lady.

"Damn." Slipped from Cassidy's lips as he stood in the doorway and watched as Key slept. She had one leg straight and the other was bent and pushed up towards her torso. The covers were sprawled across the top of her body, but the bottom half was bare. Dragging his tongue across his bottom lip, he eased the door shut and locked it, careful not to wake her up.

Pulling his shirt over his head he leaned down so that his face was aligned with her pussy. Grabbing her ass cheek he lifted it up to give him better access to her. The soft smell of *Dove Purely Pampering* soap hit his nose and caused him to lick his lips before he drug his tongue from her clit to her opening and then he took a dip in.

"Ummmm." Key thought she was dreaming that Cassidy was giving her head. She tooted her ass up in the air and allowed her mind to take her on a ride, but little did she know it wasn't a dream, it was very much her reality.

"That's it baby girl, toot that thang up for daddy." Cassidy dove head first and latched on to her clit causing her eyes to pop open. Looking over her shoulder, she tried to move from his grasp, but he had already had a taste and he was addicted to the taste of her. "Where you going?" Cassidy realized that she was woke and threw her leg over so that she was on her back and her pussy was in his face. "You didn't wake me up for breakfast, so a nigga hungry as fuck."

"You were sleeping so... oh God." She couldn't even get her words out because he was devouring her like she was his favorite meal. It had been a while since someone had ate her out like this and she wanted to feel all of it, which was why she pushed her legs all the way back, as far as they could go. "What are you doing to me?" she moaned as his thick tongue assaulted her clit.

The way he feasted on her took Key to a different level sexually, her body had never felt that high from a man's touch. It was like he was reading her mind, if she thought he needed to move over a little he was there before the thought even got all the way across her mind.

Cassidy didn't read her mind; he just studied her body. If her hips moved slightly to the left, he knew that he needed to move to the left to give her the feeling that she was longing for. If she force-fed him her pussy then he wasn't sucking hard enough, and if she pulled back, he needed to ease up some. Key had never had a man that was so in tune with her body.

"Ssss shit Cas, that feels so good," she moaned as she arched her back, threw her head back and grabbed the sheets and balled them up in her hands.

Cassidy's fingers melted into her meaty ass as he pulled her to him, "Stop running, it's only gone make it worse." He taunted, the warmth of his breath and his lips moving against her clit had her on the verge of coming and he knew it. "What's wrong baby?"

"St—Stop teasing me fuck!" She said breathless.

"Or what?" That was it, her leg began to lightly shake as she felt the flutters in the pit of her gut. Cassidy took that as the green light to go in on her. He covered her pussy with his mouth and sucked and slurped until she locked her legs around his head and brought him into her. That didn't stop or slow him down as he latched on her clit and softly nibbled.

"Oh my God, yes baby yes!" She moaned out loudly. "Shit Cas, shit!" She couldn't formulate a complete sentence if she tried. "Oh God, oh God, I'm coming." She squeezed her eyes shut as she released everything that she had pent up into his mouth and he didn't leave a drop.

"Damn you taste good." He said against her pussy sending a chill down her spine. Unable to contain himself any more. Cassidy freed himself from his pants and stood up over the bed. Looking down at her, he wiped his goatee off with the back of his hands. "You good?"

"I don't know," she said honestly. Her legs felt like spaghetti noodles and her body was twitching and she had no control over it. Cassidy chuckled at his handy work.

"Well you need to figure it out because what I'm about to do next is gonna elevate you even more." He hovered over her and kissed her lips; she pulled his bottom one into her mouth and lightly sucked tasting herself.

"Ummmm," she moaned.

"Let me find out you my little freak." She smiled and pulled him into her and invaded his mouth with her tongue.

His dick had a mind of its own as it poked away until it found the moistness, sliding in they took in a deep breath and held it as he moved slowly in and out of her until he fully fit. Key was tight, wet and warm just like he liked it.

"Oh sssssss." She hissed as he moved his body in a circular motion stretching her out just a little. "Damn." Biting down on her bottom lip, Key looked up at Cassidy who was doing the same thing trying not to let loose inside her.

"Yo pussy is lit," he said seriously. "Ummm got damn." He pulled out and then eased back in grinding into her. "I'm trying not to go in on this shit but it's hard." He was talking more to himself, he wanted to take his time before he beat it up but the way she wrapped around him was making it that much harder.

"Maybe that's the way I like it." Key taunted and Cassy nodded his head placing her knees by her ears and leaning over her in the push up position while he moved in and out of her at an even pace. "Oh ummm oh." She moaned over and over until they both exploded together. Trying to catch their breath, Cassidy rolled over onto his back. Key straightened her legs out and turned her head to look at Cassidy who was staring at the ceiling. "You do know that dick is mine, right?"

Cassidy turned his head to see if she was joking and there

wasn't a hint of humor in her face and he didn't feel any. She was serious and she wanted him to know it. Cassidy chuckled and nodded his head.

"I think I can give you that." He laid back down and looked up in the ceiling. "I just need one thing."

"What's that?"

"Honesty, I hate surprises, so I need you to keep it real with me at all times. Even if you think it's insignificant."

"I think I can do that." She leaned over and placed her head on his chest. "When are you going back to the hospital?"

"I don't know, I gotta meet my brothers in a few. I was supposed to been up and moving but I was tired as fuck." Cassidy glanced down at her and couldn't deny the feeling of peace and completeness.

"So you gotta few minutes to spare?" She raised her brows.

"Yeah what's up?" She smirked and bit into her bottom lip as she slid down his torso until her mouth was over his dick.

"I just wanted to tell you a little something-something," she whispered into his dick causing it to jump. Twirling her tongue around his head and then swallowed him whole. Cassidy gasped and lifted his head up to watch her take all of him and pull it out and then stick it all the way back in not forgetting to suck in on the way out. Cassidy shook his head; she was exactly what he needed.

CHAPTER FIVE

Never Again

Kahleno watched as AD paced the floor of his living room. He had showed up at his house a few minutes after he had gotten off the phone with Cassidy. His whole aura was off, and he couldn't tell if it was because his mother was in the hospital or it was because of something else. As bad as he wanted to pry, he knew that he couldn't because it would just push him away.

"Baby." Icelynn's soft voice entered the room before she did, and it instantly stopped AD where he stood. Just her presence brought so much peace in his life and he welcomed it. Turning to her, he moved in her direction swiftly.

"How's baby girl?" Was the first words out of his mouth.

"She's good, I just got her to sleep good enough for me to

come check on you." The weary look in her eyes had Kahleno on edge and when Sutton walked in with tears in her eyes, he knew something else was up. "Thank you so much Kahleno for letting us crash here for a little."

"No thanks needed." He shot quickly at Icelynn before he turned to his brother. "The fuck going on? I tried to chill but I don't like this." Kahleno stated honestly. "Holla at me bruh."

AD looked at Icelynn who immediately got teary eyed, when Sutton made her way to her friend and the two began crying together. AD's hands shook with anticipation of ending Salem and Dimples lives, but he couldn't do anything until he knew his girls were safe.

"Bro ride with me." AD said and Icelynn looked up from Sutton's shoulder.

"No I'm going." She said with eagerness in her tone.

AD knew that this was going to be a fight, but he couldn't let her subject her mental to something like that. Killing Salem, no matter how dirty he did her, would scar her for life and selfishly, he didn't want that. He wanted to ensure that their life was smooth and filled with happiness from this day forward.

"Come here baby." He reached for her and she went to him. Enclosing her in his arms, he inhaled deeply as he took in the essence of her. Everything that she was, he wanted to experience, and he knew that if he allowed her to even be in the same room, he would lose out on that opportunity.

"Adoreé you can't take this from me," she cried into his chest.

"Baby I know what he did to you, to Isis but this ain't you. Something like this has the potential to taint the person you are, and a nigga can't have that. I need you in a way I've never needed anybody. Your mind, body and soul. You weren't built for this kind of shit and I'm not trying to lose you up here," he lightly tapped her head, "just because you wanted revenge. That's what I'm here for. I promise you that nigga will never hurt you again and I put that on my life." He ran his hands through her hair causing her eyes to close and take in the words that he was saying. "I need you to trust me," he said when his eyes were on hers again.

"Okay," she said barely above a whisper.

Even though she wanted to fight what he said he was right. The rage flowing through her may have gotten her there, but she wasn't vicious enough of a person to actually pull the trigger. She would have beat the hell out of him but to actually kill him, she didn't know if she could. Then again, the thoughts of what he could have been doing to her daughter may have drove her there, but would she be able to live with that decision. For that reason alone, she was going to listen to her man and let him handle it.

"Thank you for trusting me." AD kissed her on the forehead and looked at Kahleno who was still looking back and forth trying to figure out what was going on. "If baby girl wake up before I get back, call me aight?"

"Okay." Icelynn leaned up and kissed his lips before taking a seat on the couch where she was joined by Sutton.

"You riding bro?" AD asked and Kahleno didn't say

anything, he just leaned down and kissed Suttons lips and told her he would be right back. She nodded her head with tears still in her eyes at what Icelynn had just told her. She couldn't believe that they had went through that on top of what happened to Siya.

The two brothers left, the car ride to where they were going was silent for the most part. Kahleno's patience was wearing very thin. He could feel his brother's energy and it was off, he was on alert, but he didn't know why and that bothered him.

"You gone tell me what's up or am I busting blind?" Kahleno said looking straight out the window. He was trying his best to give his brother the benefit of the doubt, but he was making it hard.

"The nigga I was shooting at last night was Icelynn's ex." AD glanced at his brother and then back at the road. Kahleno didn't say anything he just waited for him to continue, there had to be more for them to act like that. "When we left the restaurant, we went back to her house to check on Isis, but he had snatched her from the house." Kahleno's head snapped to AD.

"Say what now?"

"Yeah, Icelynn went crazy. He fucked the babysitter up and threw her in the laundry room. Him and Dimples' dumb ass."

"The stripper you were banging from Onyx?" AD nodded his head. "What the fuck you do? You kill that bitch in public? Please don't tell me you did no bullshit like that?"

Kahleno knew that AD was a hot head and if he was mad, there wasn't much that he would care about other than taking that anger out on someone. Something as serious as a kid getting taken, that would definitely send him over the edge.

"Nah, but that bitch told him where Icelynn lived and then had the nerve to show up at the restaurant with him smiling and shit. Then the dumb bitch didn't have the smarts to get out of town. She went back to her job like she didn't know who the fuck I was."

"Stupid bitch," Kahleno gritted.

"Icelynn beat the hell out of her and we made her tell us where that nigga was, and he was at her crib." AD shook his head. "When we get there, Isis runs out of the room screaming with her little night gown raised up."

"The fuck? That's his fucking daughter."

"He ain't shit but food for Cassidy's fat ass hogs," AD growled. Isis was his baby and there wasn't anyone that could tell him any different.

"You know what the fuck I mean nigga, calm yo hostile ass down."

"We keep asking her if he touched her and she keeps saying no but he tried. She said she fought him off. The way she's acting, won't let me out of her sight, is telling me that something did happen, and she just don't want us to know."

"Yeah y'all may need to take her to see someone. Shit like that can really fuck up a kid's mental and you don't want her carrying that shit around," Kahleno said.

AD remained quiet because he knew the lengths that

carrying something like that around takes you. He was still battling with those same demons and he didn't want that for Isis. Thankful for Icelynn, he had made an appointment to see Dr. Reems within the next week, but he was thinking that they needed to make it a family thing since Isis had been through this.

"I wanted to kill that nigga so fucking bad." Kahleno didn't miss the change in conversation but he decided not to speak on it. "If Isis wasn't right there on my hip I would have. I couldn't let her see that side of me, I wouldn't have been able to live with myself if my baby girl was scared of me."

"Yeah you did the right thing." Kahleno nodded. "So where that nigga at?"

"That's where we about to go. I told clean up and Spiff to bring that nigga to his warehouse since the farm house was surrounded."

"Fuck! We gotta head over there when we leave here. I called Cassidy's bitch ass before we left the house and he didn't answer. I guess he'll meet us there and I'll have to fill him in." AD nodded his head as he pulled into the warehouse and parked around back.

Walking in all you could smell was piss and weed. Walking in Spiff was sitting at the table looking like he could fall asleep at any minute, but it didn't stop him from smoking blunts to the face.

"Where that bitch at?" AD's voiced boomed causing a beat-up Salem to look his way. He was hanging from the ceiling by a metal chain. Spiff had that installed the first time one of the guys came up short with their money.

"She wouldn't shut the fuck up, so I put her ass in the freezer." He ashed the blunt that was hanging from the corner of his mouth and pointed to the back of the warehouse and AD laughed for the first time.

"Nigga the bitch probably froze to death before I could put a bullet up her rotten ass pussy and blow that shit away."

"Damn nigga, that's some shit that I wanted to see, too. Let me go get her. I ain't never seen no shit like that before." Spiff said moving towards the back of the warehouse and Kahleno shook his head at AD and Spiff. He walked over to Salem and stared at him for a second.

He couldn't understand how a man would want to hurt a child, his child. That was enough to piss him off, so he cocked back and slammed his fist into the side of Salem's jaw so hard it spun him around on the chain a few times before he came back face to face with him.

"You should have stayed your bitch ass in Chicago." AD's tone was evil, and he didn't try and hide it.

He was having a hard time controlling himself, but it wasn't working because the minute Salem's bloody smile spread across his face AD lost it. He walked over to where he was and started giving him chest shots.

AD was hitting him over and over in the same spot until he heard a bone crack and it was only then that he moved on to another spot doing the same thing. Blood quickly filled

Salem's lungs making it difficult for him to breathe, one of his ribs had punctured it.

"What's that nigga, I can't hear you," AD said taking off the shit that he had on and standing before Salem with a mug on his handsome face. "Talk that shit that you were talking in the restaurant muthafucka." AD hit him with an upper cut.

"Ahhh please let me go! Please!" Dimples cried as Spiff drug her through the warehouse by her hair. Her arms and feet were still tied, and she was just screaming her heart out. She was hoping that someone would come in and save her but the minute she laid eyes on AD she knew that it would never happen.

"Shut up bitch before I slit your throat, then I'm gone be mad cause I wanna see this shit that AD about to do." Spiff said as he threw Dimples at AD's feet and went around the table and sat down and grabbed the blunt that he had put out.

"The fuck is wrong with y'all?" Kahleno said looking back and forth between AD and Spiff, they watched too much TV. All these inventive ways to kill people was foreign to Kahleno he was satisfied with shooting them in the head and walking away.

"Please AD don't do this. I saved the little girl, I walked in the room and he had his hands down her little panties and I stopped him." AD froze, the sound of his heart beat echoed in his ear and he closed his eyes and prayed that nothing happened to her.

"Did he—" he couldn't even let the words leave his mouth.

"No I stopped him before he did. That should count for something right?" Dimples pleaded.

AD pulled a pocket knife that he had in his pocket, he normally kept it in the car, but he grabbed it before he came in. Flipping it open he cut the ropes that bound Dimples arms and legs. She got up on her knees and the minute she opened her mouth to say thank you, AD backhanded her, and blood spewed from her mouth.

"Bitch you led him there," AD said as he kicked her in the face. If Siya knew that he was putting his hands on a woman she would probably knock him upside the head, but right now his morals weren't a factor in his decision to cause bodily harm to Dimples. "You mad over some dick that don't belong to you, so you put a seven-year-old baby in danger you stupid bitch." AD drove the knife in his hand through her heart.

"Ahhhhhhhh!" Dimples screamed out in pain. Taking the nine that he had tucked in his waist he pulled it out and roughly spread her legs apart.

"You wanted to fuck that bad that you would feed a little girl to a fucking pimp." AD growled as he pushed back the small t-shirt dress that she wore up her stomach and shoved the gun inside her and let off two rounds instantly killing Dimples.

It was like AD was in a daze as he stood up over her, placed his foot on her chest, pulled the knife out of her and wiped it on her dress before he stood and walked over to Salem who was barely hanging on.

His breaths were short and shallow, and that satisfied AD.

He took the knife and repeatedly stabbed Salem until he was lifeless. When he looked at him, he was satisfied with his handy work and without another word he walked over to the table and grabbed the blunt that Spiff was handing him.

"No one will ever hurt them again, and I put that on my life," was all AD said while they waited for clean-up to come through.

CHAPTER SIX

£et's Ride Out

"Girl I'm so damn sorry." Key hugged Icelynn.
After Cassidy finally called his brothers back,
Kahleno filled him in on what was going on with AD and
Icelynn. Key felt so bad for her and couldn't imagine having to
go through that. She as glad that Kane's father wasn't in his
life.

"I'm just glad she's okay." Icelynn sniffed and grabbed the
cup of coke that she had and took a sip from it. The door bell
rung and pulled them all from their thoughts. Sutton got up
and went to answer it.

She looked through the peep hole and it was Karson.
Despite Kahleno's reservations she had kept open communication with her on the strength of Kahlil. She wanted him to
see the two of them getting along for his sake. She called and

told her what happened to Siya and Kahlil wanted to be with his dad and Sutton so she said that she could bring him.

"Hey," Sutton said and pulled the door open and stepped aside for them to come in. Kahlil hugged Sutton tightly, she leaned down and kissed the top of his head.

"Where's Isis?" he asked noticing Icelynn walking to the door. She heard a female voice at the door, and she wanted to make sure that her pregnant friend was okay.

"She's in the back with Kane." Icelynn pointed to the back of the house where the game room was. Kahlil's little face balled up as he looked back and forth between Sutton and Icelynn.

"Who the fuck is Kane and why is he back there with my woman?" Kahlil tilted his head to the side and Icelynn had to walk off to keep from laughing.

"Kahlil Maler!" Sutton yelled before Karson could open her mouth. She was about to school Sutton on correcting her son like he was hers but the look that she delivered told her to keep her comment to herself.

"Sorry, I'm trying man." Kahlil tucked his little head down and Sutton couldn't resist kneeling down to coddle him.

"You remember what we talked about?" she said softly while kissing his cheek and he nodded his head and smiled.

"You still love me?" he cheesed real big making Sutton laugh and shake her head.

"I'll always love you more." Kahlil hugged her neck and took off down the hall where the other kids were. "You can come in."

"No that's okay." Karson's tone was defeated. She was still getting use to the fact that there was no more her and Kahleno. Even though they had been separated for a while she still hung on to the thought of them. Now standing at his front door, the door that she had walked in freely at one point, being invited in by another woman was bothering her.

She wasn't about to start anything because she knew that it wouldn't end well for her and she had actually met a guy that she really liked. When she talked to Sutton at the shop, she meant everything that she said she just couldn't help the pang of jealousy that shot through her every time she saw her. She made a promise to herself to stay away until she could get that under control.

"Okkkayyyy," Sutton said starting to feel like what Kahleno said about her little speech being bullshit. Sutton was all about forgiving these days, but she wasn't about to be out looking stupid either. Before she could voice her concerns, Karson opened her mouth again.

"I've got an appointment." Karson smiled nervously, she was lying, and she didn't want it to come off as such. "Is Siya okay?" Karson asked, even though they had been through their little issues as of lately she still cared about Siya. She was Kahlil's grandmother and she didn't hate the woman she just wished she would stay out of Kahleno's affairs.

"I've got faith that she will be." Sutton smiled, she had called Mega a while ago and he said that her stats showed that the therapy was actually working, and he was grateful. "She had to have some kind of Oxygen Therapy to slow down the effects of the smoke inhalation on her nervous system. She'll come out of that tonight so we'll no more but she's gonna be fine."

"Good, good. Kahlil would go crazy without his mawmaw." Karson rolled her eyes playfully.

"Girl yes!" Sutton laughed and then an uncomfortable silence fell between the two.

Karson cleared her throat. "Well I'm gonna go and head out so I can make it to my appointment on time."

"Aight girl I'll keep you posted." Sutton went to shut the door and Karson stopped her. "What's up?"

"Thank you for being an adult even when I wasn't. It's still a little hard for me but I'm coming around," Karson told her truthfully. Sutton didn't say anything, and she didn't need her to, she wanted her to know how she truly felt.

Sutton could have been a total bitch, and with the way that Kahleno feels about her, she could have possibly made her life a living hell, but she didn't. That made Karson look at Sutton in a different light. She would still have to get use to her opening Kahleno's door like she owned it and disciplining her son but that would come with time.

Now she just needed to stop creating storms for herself starting with her next stop after leaving here. It's time to tell her baby's father that he's gonna be a daddy. She would just keep how it happened to herself.

Sutton shut the door and returned to the living room. She didn't say anything she just thought about what Karson said and shook her head. She had a feeling that she wasn't done with her bullshit yet, but she hoped that for Kahlil's sake that she was.

"Everything okay?" Key asked looking skeptical. She heard a female's voice at the door and when her friend came back, she had a weird look on her face, that put her friends on alert. Sutton was pregnant and couldn't fight her battles but the both of them were ready for whatever.

"Yeah girl I ain't worried about that." Sutton waved her hands. "Her mouth is saying that everything is okay, and she respects my place in Kahleno and Kahlil's life, but her body language is saying something totally different. Plus, when were at the doctor Kahlil said something about her dating a cop that knew Kahleno." The girls gasped. "Exactly so—"

Click! Click! The room fell silent as the girls looked around from where the sound came from, with everything that was going on with the men that they cared about, they were on high alert. The barrel of the rifle met them before he did and when he did Sutton stretched her eyes wide.

"Who the fuck hurt my girl?" Kahlil said barely able to hold the aerosol rifle. It was almost the size of him. *Click! Click!* He pumped the barrel a few more times. "Why ain't no one tell me?"

"Yo he stupid," Kane said walking in with Isis right behind him. He had a smirk on his face as he looked at Kahlil holding the bb gun.

Isis had her arms crossed across her chest with the meanest little mug, she felt like Kahlil was doing the most. She was appreciative that he felt the need to protect her, he was just extremely extra with it. That on top of the fact that him and Kane had been into it since the moment he walked in the door had irritated her. All she wanted to do was chill and wait for her AD to get back from wherever he went.

"Call me stupid again bitch." Kahlil pointed the bb gun in Kane's direction who grilled him. The two couldn't get along for anything, it was like they fought over the smallest things.

"Kahlil, first off if you say another curse word, I'm taking your phone, tablet, and your Xbox." Sutton pointed at him, but his attention was on Kane who wore a smirk on his face.

"Yeah nigga curse again," he laughed.

"Kane you want ya ass beat?" Key glared at him and he rolled his eyes.

"He about to get his a—tail beat." Kahlil caught himself and brought the bb gun up to his eyes like he was getting his aim. Sutton snatched it from his hands and then glared at him.

"What are you doing with this anyway? I hate that Kahleno bought this for you." She walked to the door where the basement was and walked down the stairs, locking the bb gun in the gun cabinet with the real guns.

"That's what you get punk." Kane leaned in so that only Kahlil and Isis could hear him because they were all standing close.

"Keep talking, bitch nigga," Kahlil said through clenched teeth. He had heard his uncle Cassidy call plenty of people bitch niggas and he always thought it sounded cool and he was excited for a reason to use it.

"I bet you won't swing." Kane took a step towards Kahlil. Kahlil smirked and then swung and punched Kane in the mouth. Kane countered quickly with a shot to Kahlil's eye. The two started swinging at each other like they were in a boxing ring. Somehow, they ended up on the floor, each taking a turn to get the best of the other one.

"Kane cut that out!" Key yelled getting up from her seat right as Sutton walked up from the basement. "What are you doing? I can't take you nowhere!" she fussed as she pulled them apart.

"Kahlil that's it, you are on punishment!" Sutton yelled as she headed in the direction of the fight.

"Just let them fight geesh," Isis said securing her arms across her chest. "I told them earlier just fight and get it over with so they both can just shut up." She rolled her eyes and went to sit on the couch where her mother was sitting. Icelynn chastised her the minute she was by her side.

"Isis what I tell you about your got damn mouth?"

"What maaaa they're annoying," she pouted. All she wanted to do was to lay in the back and watch TV while she waited for AD to come and she couldn't even do that thanks to Beavis and Butthead.

Icelynn shook her head and went to help Key and Sutton break up the boys. She wanted to laugh so bad because the two of them were one of a kind, but they didn't even see it. Isis didn't bother to help she just wrapped her arms around herself and curled up on the couch and watched the showdown. She just hoped that this was enough to make them stop with all the foolishness.

Once the ladies got them apart, Sutton was out of breath and needed to sit down. She pulled Kahlil with her who was still trying to get at Kane.

"Stop it Kahlil!" she called out to him.

"He tried to punk me," Kahlil said grilling Sutton, his little face was so cute that it was taking a lot out of her not to laugh at him.

"Apologize Kanaan, right now!" Key yelled with Kane jacked up by his arm. He didn't want to apologize because he felt like they both hit each other so it was even. "Aight you don't want to apologize then let's take a trip to the bathroom." He knew what that meant so he opened his mouth to do what his mother said.

"Sorry Kahlil."

"You too Kahlil," Sutton urged.

"Sorry Kane." They both dropped their heads.

"Y'all ain't supposed to fight each other. If anything y'all should be getting to know each other because it looks like y'all gone be around each other a lot." Sutton said looking back and forth between the two boys. They looked at her and then back at each other before they both broke out into a smile.

"You quick with ya hands man." Kane held his hand out to call a truce. He wasn't lying either. Kahlil swung quick and hard, and proved to be the best opponent he had ever fought, and he fought a lot.

"Yeah I am." Kahlil smiled and then stuck his hand out to accept the truce. "You hit hard as hell," he said and then looked up at Sutton, "I mean heck." When he gave her his award-winning smile, she couldn't do anything but shake her head.

"Alright now go play, I don't want to hear anything else about you fighting. Got that?" Sutton yelled at both of them and they both nodded.

"Come on let's go play Fortnite," Kahlil said.

"Cool, I'm going first."

"No the hell you ain't."

"Yes I am, I beat you up, so I got first."

"Nigga you got yo ass beat."

"KAHLIL!"

"KANE!" Sutton and Key said at the same time.

"Sorry!" they mumbled along with a few other words that weren't audible. The ladies shook their heads. There was no use in wasting their breath with those two.

"Isis you want to go and play?" Icelynn asked her daughter, she seemed to be down and not herself. She had a good reason for that, but she wanted her to get back to being her. Yes, that was a lot to take in for a seven-year-old, but she was going to try her best to help her daughter get passed it.

"No, I just want to wait for AD to come back." Her tone was low, she could tell that her daughter was exhausted. Isis was scared to go to sleep because every time she did, she would see Salem and that freaked her out.

"Okay." Icelynn wiped away the tears that tried to fall.

"He'll be back soon." She pulled out her phone to send him a text. When she looked at her phone, she had a message from her mother about moving to Arizona for her job. Icelynn closed her phone because she knew for a fact that she would never be able to leave North Carolina, her heart was there.

CHAPTER SEVEN

*R*evelations

"How long y'all been here?" Mega asked the minute he stepped into Siya's room. It had been a couple days since they did the therapy. She had yet to wake up and he had been by her side the entire time.

He had just left out to go down and check on his sister. The doctor called and said that they had some new information on her condition, they wouldn't tell him anything over the phone, so he rushed down to see what they were talking about.

"We just got here about ten minutes ago," Kahleno said looking from the window that he was just staring out of. "She still ain't woke up yet?"

Mega walked to the side of his wife's bed that was free and tucked his hands in his pockets. He looked around the room and all of his sons wore the same expression, pain mixed with a little bit of determination.

"Marlin is here," Mega said before turning his attention back to his wife.

The conversation that he had with Marlin played through his mind. He had never gave him a reason to doubt him, but all of this was too much for anyone to deal with. Let alone trust the man who raised the woman who put them in this situation to begin with.

"That nigga can die too," Cassidy said leaning back in his chair. He was on the left side of his mother, further away from the door.

"I'm with him," Kahleno said and looked out the window.

"He's not here to cause trouble, he came to warn me about a few things." Mega paused to take a deep breath. Ziva was causing more trouble than they care to deal with, and he was ready to put an end to it. "Ziva came to him for help with taking ya mother and me out. She seems to think that what she went through was our fault and the fact that Marlin took my side he owed her."

"What the fuck you do to this bitch pops?" Cassidy said giving his father his full attention. "I mean damn, she's going through great lengths for a nigga that didn't give a fuck."

"When I met Ziva we were wild, I was never committed to her. Everything was about the drug game and fucking. We did all kinds of shit from threesomes to orgies. It was always a party so I'm not sure why she felt that I would ever take her serious enough to have anything with her." Mega shook his head. Just the thought about what he shared with Ziva put a bad taste in his mouth.

"The bitch sounds crazy if you ask me," Kahleno said and then looked over at AD. Even though they planned to kill her, she was still the person who brought AD into this world and they didn't want to be insensitive to that situation, but it was hard seeing where his mother lay.

"Fuck you looking at me for? I can't wait to put a bullet in her brain." AD shrugged, he tried to feel conflicted with how he wanted to handle Ziva, but it never came. The only emotion that he felt was that of anger and guilt for even letting her get into his head enough to doubt the love Siya had for him. Shit was still hard to process but he was getting there.

"I—I am your mother," Siya struggled to get out and all four men rushed to her bed. Tears stung Mega's eyes as he said a quick thank you to the man above for answering his prayers. "AD."

"Stop trying to talk ma, I'm right here." AD leaned around Cassidy so that she could see him. When she reached for him, Cassidy stepped back and let him around.

"Chill Siya let me go get the nurse." The look that she gave Mega, stopped him in his tracks. She was going to tell him what she needed to tell him, and she didn't care what anyone had to say about it.

"I—" she started coughing, Kahleno reached for the water pitcher that was beside the bed, but she waved him off. "No!" she took a few deep breaths and cleared her throat. Coughing was painful and every time she tried to talk it caused her to cough, but she didn't care. Once she finished saying what she had to say then they could all go about their business. "Ziva she—"

"Will be dead by the time you get out of here," Mega interrupted.

"No!" she yelled wanting all of them to just shut up and let her say what she needed to say. "She stole my embryos from the Cryolab." Confusion filled all of their faces, so she continued. "She paid the doctor to implant them into her, AD you came from me, I just didn't carry you. I am your mother." Tears gathered at the brim of her eyes before they spilled over onto her face.

Mega could feel the anger that'd been bellowing in his belly rise to the surface as he turned and walked towards the window that was on the far side of the room. This woman was playing with his life, with his family's life and she was going to pay.

"So all of this shit was for nothing." Mega gritted his teeth. "We created AD and she paid someone to—" he couldn't shape his lips to say something so deranged. "What the fuck!" he yelled.

"She loves you that much Mega, she wants a life with you," Siya said in a defeated tone. Mega turned to her, he could feel her trying to give up on them in her voice, but he wouldn't have it. He would take his own life at her feet before he lived without her. He loved her that much.

"Siya—"

"But she'll die by my hands before she ever gets it!" Siya said putting him out of his misery. Everything that she had been through was for this family and she'd be damned if she lay down and let anyone take that from her. "I'm tired of playing with this bitch. She almost made me lose the most important thing to me, the respect of my boys. Make her pay for that Mega or you have to answer to me." She hit her chest right before she went into a fit of coughing.

Mega's chest got tight just thinking about the anguish that his actions put his family through. This was the exact reason why he taught his sons to find a good woman and make it work with her. A woman scorned was a headache.

Nurses flooded the room and asked the men to leave. They assured them that she would be okay, but she needed to rest to get better. Mega let Siya know that he was gone be right outside.

"Your O2 is dropping, I need you to stop talking Mrs. Maler." The nurse tried to warn but Siya had something else to say.

"Tell Sutton to do that hair show or," Siya coughed a little more while the nurses tried to urge her to stop but she ignored them. "I heard h—her. She needs to go or I'm k— kicking her ass." Siya coughed more as the nurses shoed them out of the room.

They all stood on the outside of the door looking in while they worked on Siya. AD's chest was so tight that he felt like he was about to pass out. He didn't know how much his heart could take before it gave out on him.

"Son!" Mega grabbed his shoulder when he saw him grab his chest. "You need to see a doctor."

"Nah I'm good, I just—" he shook his head.

"I know son, it's like shit just won't stop. I promise you that I'm gonna take care of it. I'm sorry that I even put any of you in this position. I should have killed her way back when." Mega knew that Ziva was gone be a problem back when Marlin promised she wouldn't.

"This shit is just too got damn much. I just need it to be over." AD was more confused than ever about who he was.

"My blood is running through you; your mother's blood is running through you. That shit Ziva was talking about was irrelevant. I can't even be mad at her for that shit because she did us a favor." Mega slid his hands in his pockets and leaned his back against the wall. "After Kahleno we had trouble conceiving. Your mother and I wanted a house full of kids and it depressed her that we couldn't. So we went to a doctor that helps you get pregnant. They took my sperm and her eggs and made little embryos. They take the embryos and put them inside the woman and the woman grows the baby. Simply put." He shrugged his shoulders.

"So I was a got damn science experiment?" AD stared at his father, no one said anything. He wasn't upset with his parents; he was more so upset with the situation. It was like, right when he got comfortable with one situation another came and knocked him back down and he didn't know how much he could take.

"You are our son, always have been." Mega sighed as he

took a step towards his son. "This shit is a mess and I won't pretend that it's not, but I also won't pretend that I'm not happy it worked out like it did. Ziva is a woman that you don't want to be attached to, trust me." Pulling his son in for a hug he sighed. "We are a family; we are the Maler family."

AD's body was stiff as a board as confusion swam around his mind. One part of him felt a sense of relief knowing that Siya was really his mother by blood but it still bothered him that all of this was going on in the first place.

"I'm good pop." AD finally returned the embrace and the two men patted each other on the back. AD looked up and right into the eyes of Siya, she was watching the men the whole time the doctors worked on her. She prayed that the news of her being his biological mother eased the tension within the family. When AD offered up a small smile that put Siya's mind and heart at ease and she finally laid back and let them do whatever they needed to do with her.

"I feel ya, I'm here for whatever and everything will work out." Mega slipped his hands in his pockets and turned towards the door and watched as they got Siya back comfortable in the bed.

"No it won't not until that bitch is in the ground," AD said to his father's back. Mega turned around with the deepest scowl and nodded his head.

"Indeed son." Then he turned and watched his wife as he thought about everything that he wanted to do to Ziva.

CHAPTER EIGHT

*S*howtime

"I feel so bad even being here with Siya in the hospital and I feel even worse that you're here with me." Sutton wined as she rubbed her stomach that was barely there. She was safely out of the first trimester and entering her fourteenth week of pregnancy with ease and the two of them couldn't be happier.

Stress seemed to surround them, and Sutton tried her best not to let things get her worked up, but it was hard. Especially when the people you love the most were getting hurt. She knew that stress wasn't good for the baby and for that reason she went the extra mile to remain calm.

"Well ma said if you didn't do it, she was gone kick yo ass so it's up to you." That sexy smirk that Sutton had grown to love so much spread across Kahleno's handsome chocolate face as he shrugged his shoulders. "So you can go out there and show them why you're the best at what you do or take that shit up with Siya Maler."

"I just love that lady." Sutton smiled with tears in her eyes. The thought of losing Siya pained her more than she led on. Siya had become a mother figure in her life, something that she needed more than ever right now. She needed guidance going into this next chapter in her life and Siya was always there for her. "How is she? I need to get over there tomorrow."

"She's okay, they had to up her oxygen because her little hardheaded ass won't shut the fuck up." Kahleno shook his head because even with the coughing spells, she was still in there trying to talk until Mega gave them permission to give her something to relax. Siya hated that and cursed him out until she finally passed out.

"You know I'm telling her you said that, right?" Sutton gave him the side eyes and again Kahleno smirked. He eased up behind her and allowed his semi hard dick to rest on her ass as he leaned down and placed a kiss on her collar bone causing her to moan out unintentionally.

"And if you do, I swear to make you pay for it," he whispered in her ear and she bit down on her bottom lip as her eyes rolled to the back of her head. Her mind drifted back to the love making session that they had before they got there.

"Well in that case let me make a phone call." She winked at him over her shoulder and then forced herself to pull away from him. She felt the most comfortable in his arms and she hardly ever wanted to leave the sanctity of them.

When she tried to walk off, he pulled her back to him and he pressed his lips against hers. Kahleno's tongue invaded her mouth and they explored each other. Butterflies settled in the pit of Sutton's stomach as her hard nipples poked him in the chest. This pregnancy had her horny to the point she could barely control it.

"Fuck!" Kahleno pulled away from the love of his life and adjusted himself. He was mad that they had gotten something started and they were unable to finish. "Oh you taking care of this when we get home so save some got damn energy."

Sutton could hear the frustration in his voice, she giggled and leaned up and pecked him on the lips again. She winked at him letting him know that she had him. Satisfied with her gesture he headed to the back to look for his brothers and his son.

"Hey, tell the kids I'll be back there in a minute to get them situated for the show." Sutton yelled to Kahleno's back. He nodded his head letting her know that he heard her and kept moving towards the back.

Piper sat off to the side and watched the exchange between Sutton and Kahleno. She was truly happy that Sutton had gotten out of the dead-end relationship with Trouble and found her a real man. She didn't think she's ever seen Sutton this happy and honestly it looked good on her.

The love between Sutton and Kahleno was so real, and it showed all over Sutton. Piper wished that they could share their happiness together but the strain on their friendship wouldn't allow that. Piper didn't understand why they were still at odds with each other if she wasn't even with Trouble anymore. She hoped that now that she was happy maybe she would be more open to having a civil conversation.

"Girl I know you better not go over there," Sunny said noticing that Piper was looking in the direction of Sutton by the DJ booth. She knew that if Sutton and Piper got together that there was a chance for her to spill the beans on her and Saque's *friendship*. "She's played you on more than one occasion and at this point you look kind of desperate." She turned her nose up at Piper who sighed heavily.

Sunny rubbed her stomach and glared in the direction of Sutton. Hate burned within her when her man walked back out and asked her if she was okay and handed her a bottle of water. Why couldn't she find someone to treat her like that? She thought she had that with Trouble, but he showed her on more than one occasion that that was not the case.

Speaking of Trouble no one had seen nor heard from him lately. Even Sunny had been calling and looking around for him. Sunny thought that it was strange that no one had seen or heard from him. Even though she was on her mission to find her next sponsor for her and her kids, she didn't want anything bad to happen to Trouble but she felt like it already had. He had a serious gambling problem and she knew that it was only a matter of time before it caught up to him.

"It's not desperate, I just miss my friend," Piper admitted.

"Damn so what the fuck am I? Chopped liver? The fuck?" Sunny asked truly offended.

Minus trying to steal her man, Sunny had been a good friend to Piper. She helped her around the shop as much as she could without her back hurting. Sunny was always a listening ear when Piper wanted to vent about issues that her and Saque may have had. Granted, she used that information to her advantage, but she still listened.

"Girl it ain't even like that and this ain't about you. That's been my friend for years and I miss her. It has nothing to do with the relationship that I have with you." Piper rolled her eyes and headed in the direction of Sutton and Kahleno who had rejoined her.

Kahleno said something in Sutton's ear making her giggle like a school girl. She shook her head and threw her head back and he placed a soft kiss on her neck. Piper smiled at the two while she could hear Sunny kissing her teeth from behind her.

"You need to hurry up, Kahlil and Kane back here tearing shit up," Kahleno said when Piper was in ear shot. When his eye's met Piper's his face became serious. He knew the history between the two and he wasn't feeling his wife arguing while she was pregnant with his seed.

He felt the tension the minute Piper was close enough to touch and he wasn't feeling it. He wanted Sutton to be as stress free as possible and he would do anything to make sure that happened.

Kahleno's eyes held a hint of evil and Piper had to break eye contact soon after joining. She knew what kind of man he was, and she wasn't trying to start any drama. She just wanted her friend back and hoped that they could have a quick conversation.

"Take that bullshit on somewhere, she pregnant and she ain't about to be arguing about a muthafucking thing," Kahleno voiced. "Cause if something happens to my kids it's gone be some hymn singing and flower bringing, and I put that on everything." Kahleno's tone was calm and low, from the outside looking in you would never know that he had just threatened her life.

Swallowing hard Piper nodded her head, she wrung her hands together while she tried to put together her thoughts. "I come in peace." She offered up a small smile that wasn't returned. She was starting to think that maybe Sunny was right and she was playing herself trying to talk to Sutton.

"It's okay baby." Sutton turned to Kahleno and patted his chest to get his attention because he was staring a hole through Piper, like he wanted to rip her head off. "Kahleno!"

"No! I don't want to hear that shit and I know how you are and you ain't got time to be stressing over no bullshit. Fuck that!" he was getting pissed by the second and Piper knew that she just should have left but she just wanted to see her friend.

"Congratulations on the baby." Piper's words felt genuine and it lowered the guard that Kahleno had up but not enough to erase the scowl on his handsome face.

"Babies." Sutton beamed placing her hands on her stomach.

"Oh my God Sutton that's amazing, with your fertile ass."
Piper joked and Sutton laughed, further easing that tension
that surrounded the group. "I'm so damn happy for y'all! Like
y'all are damn sure couple goals." Piper nodded with the
widest smile. "Like you're glowing Sut, everything around you
is glowing."

"Thanks, yeah like life is too short to be anything but
happy." Her words were true, she looked back at Kahleno and
he leaned down to kiss her lips. He gave her a warning look
before he decided to walk off and let the two talk, but he
wouldn't be far and the minute he heard her voice raise one
octave above normal he was flipping the fuck out. "I don't
know what to do with that man sometimes."

"It's crazy that we both got out of fucked up relationships
and found our forever." Piper wrapped her arms around
herself and rubbed up and down her arms.

Sutton looked at her and wanted to shout to the roof top
that Saque was a fuck boy and was fucking her over and she
didn't even know it. She knew that Piper would never believe
it even with proof, so she didn't waste her breath. Then the
petty side of her wanted to do to Piper what she did to her
and let her walk around being a fool.

"Yeah, I can't wait to meet these little monsters in here
and I pray they are nothing like their brother." Sutton
laughed. Even though she was skeptical about speaking to
Piper she had to admit that it felt good talking to her. It
wouldn't change how she felt or how she viewed Piper but
talking to her felt good.

"How's your dad taking everything?" Piper knew how Sutton's father was with her dating drug dealers.

"It took him a little while but he's okay with it. Him and Kahleno are really cool." Sutton nodded her head right as Cassidy walked up with his arm around Key. He looked back and forth between Sutton and Piper with an eyebrow raised.

"Sup sis, you good?"

"Yeah Cas I'm straight." Sutton playfully rolled her eyes and Cassidy lightly mushed her making her and Key laugh. "Where the hell y'all been, the boys been back there showing out." Sutton pointed at them and then looked at Key's disheveled hair. "Y'all been fucking!" Sutton covered her mouth.

"Damn Sut tell everybody." Key grilled her before she burst out laughing.

When they got there Cassidy started with his shit, since the first time they had sex they couldn't keep their hands off of each other. The connection they had with each other before was magnified times ten and they both were excited about building together. It was all happening fast but they both welcomed it.

"Man I ain't fooling with y'all, I'm going to find my brother." Cassidy waved them off.

"Check on Kane while you're back there too!" Key yelled to his back.

"Oh my bad, Piper this is my friend Akiya, but we call her Key and Key this is Piper." Sutton introduced the two with a smile on her face.

A pain shot through Piper's heart as she introduced the Key girl as her friend and Piper as just Piper. She couldn't help the surge of jealousy that made its way through her heart. She felt like she was really losing Sutton's friendship and as hard as she tried to pretend that she didn't need it, she did. Sutton was always her voice of reasoning and now she didn't have that.

That and the fact that she had come with Cassidy pissed her off even more. She couldn't deny the same attraction that she felt that night he pulled her away from the fight at the barn, was still there. It was something about his tall frame and his broad shoulders that always had her picturing him on top of her moving in and out of her.

What the hell am I talking about? Saque is my man and he is equally sexy, and he fucks me like no other, Piper thought to herself as she shook the thoughts of Cassidy out of her mind even though his cologne still lingered, teasing her.

"Nice to meet you Piper." Key stuck her hand out, but Piper just looked at it and turned to walk off, but she ran right into something hard and then hit the ground. "Well that was fucking rude!"

Key was pissed that the bitch was trying to be smart. She couldn't help but to laugh when it backfired, and she fell on her ass. Key bent over laughing but when she stood back up and came face to face with Saque, her ex and Kane's father, her laughter was brought to a halt.

Key took a step back and stumbled herself against the DJ table. She knew that her ex was out of jail and she often prayed that they never crossed path's again. She would have been fine if she never saw him again, but here he was.

The two grilled each other, just looking in the eyes of the man that tried to take her life angered her. Normally she aimed to keep Vinny out of her business but right now she wished that her brother was here. Vinny wanted Saque in the worst way and Key just may let him have his way if the opportunity presented itself.

"Baby!" Piper yelled trying to get Saque's attention, but his mind was on the woman that ruined him. The woman that took five years of his life because she couldn't keep her legs closed. The woman that he hated to still have feelings for. The woman who broke his heart. "Saque?"

"Key? You look like you're about to cry, are you okay?" Sutton asked her friend truly concerned. It was like someone placed a black cloud over where they stood. The mood was just that gloomy and it was starting to freak Sutton out. "You want me to get Cassidy?"

Key didn't say anything; she couldn't believe that this man was standing in front of her. She couldn't imagine what would happen if he saw Kane. *Kane!* Key thought to herself as she turned around and took off around the back of the building where her son was. She had to leave this place and she prayed that Sutton understood.

"I told you she wasn't your friend," Saque fumed.

Seeing Akiya had fucked his head up and he couldn't quite put the pieces together. His thoughts and feelings were all over the place. He wanted to know how her and Sutton knew each other and he had a feeling that she did this on purpose. She was that kind of girl according to what Piper said.

Plus, Sutton was the person who held all the cards in her hand, so getting Piper to see that she was a snake would work in his favor right now. He knew that she knew about him and Sunny and this was the perfect way to turn this all around. Sutton knowing Akiya made him dislike her even more. Piper needed to stay away from them both.

"What the fuck is going on?" Sutton hissed glowering at Saque.

Seeing Key that upset and running off the way she did pissed her off and she was determined to get to the bottom of it. The way this coward was looking at her right now rubbed her the wrong way and she had half the mind to go and get Kahleno.

"Saque what the hell is going on?" Piper asked. She didn't know what was going on but whatever it was Saque wasn't happy about it. "How do you know that girl?" fear settled in Pipers belly as she held her breath and waited for him to answer her.

"Can't you see she's doing this on purpose!" Saque yelled louder than he intended to avoiding Piper's question. Seeing Akiya in front of him, pissed him off and he couldn't control himself. "She's doing business with my hoe ass ex to get back at you for not telling her that her nigga was cheating."

"Do you know how stupid you sound?" Sutton said through gritted teeth.

"So you trying to tell me that you didn't know that Akiya

was my ex, the one who had me locked up?" Saque grilled her. "I find that shit real hard to believe."

"I really don't give a fuck what you believe to be honest because what you think don't make me feel!" Sutton yelled loud enough to gain the attention of Kahleno who was making his way that way. After seeing Key as upset as she was, he knew that he needed to get up there to see what was going on with his girl. "If Key is your ex that has nothing to do with me, not that I have to explain shit to you, but my brother-in-law introduced us. I can tell you this though she's way too good for you and I'm glad she left yo retarded ass," Sutton hissed.

Kahleno stepped up behind her right as Saque called himself taking a step towards her. The look on Kahleno's face stopped him in his path and the two indulged in a stare down. Kahleno held Sutton around the waist with one hand and had the other hand by hers trying hard not to knock the clown in front of him out. When he glanced down at Piper, his stare made her shiver and she cowered behind Saque.

"The fuck I tell you?" his attention was on Piper.

"Aye don't talk to my girl like that."

"Who the fuck gone stop me?" He moved Sutton behind him and then took a step forward. Saque knew who Kahleno was, he wasn't afraid of the big bad Maler Men, but he wasn't stupid either. He knew that he didn't have the backing to go up against them, so he shook his head.

"You need to tell your girl to mind her business."

"Address her again and watch what the fuck happens."

Kahleno closed the gap a little more. He was trying not to show out at Sutton's event, but it was getting harder by the second.

"Saque let's just go." Piper knew that this situation could go from bad to worse in a matter of seconds. Kahleno stood in front of them like a raging bull, she didn't know how many more chances they had to move along but she didn't want to find out. Grabbing Saque's arm she tugged on him trying to get him away.

"She's not your got damn friend, you see that shit now." Saque didn't know how to stop and Piper was afraid that he was going to end up hurt or worse.

"Since he wants to be a bitch, did he tell you that I caught him and Sunny hugged up at Victoria Secrets a little while ago?" Sutton said trying to get around Kahleno, she was pissed and tired of Saque. Piper had always been fucked up when it came to men, but she blamed him for her new found philosophies.

"Calm the fuck down before I air this bitch out Sutton, I'm not playing. You got one more time to raise your voice then I'm gone show the fuck out and I don't care who in my line of fire." He threatened but at that point she didn't care. Piper and Saque could both catch a hot one.

"What are you talking about Sutton? Don't do that because you're upset that Saque is putting me up on game. I mean think about it, why else would you hire his ex-girlfriend? I even told you that she had him put in jail and you still do some stuff like that."

"Listen to yourself you ignorant bitch!" Sutton seethed. She was low key hurt because she never thought that there would come a day that she would think so lowly of Piper, someone she called a sister. "Did you ever tell me his bitch's name? Did you show me a picture of who she was?" Sutton glared at Piper.

Making her way around Kahleno but he had her by the waist and against him. He could tell that she was getting riled up, so he leaned down and whispered in her ear.

"Calm your little ass down before you piss me off Sutton, this the last time I'm telling you."

Piper thought about the things that were coming out of Sutton's mouth and she knew that she had never mentioned any of those things to Sutton because Saque had never mentioned them to her. He always referred to her as that bitch or the hoe, never by name.

"Exactly," Sutton said when she realized that Piper was thinking over what she asked. "After everything you saw me go through with that bitch and you openly let her into your relationship, that ain't no one's fault but your own. Stupid bitch." She said typing away at her phone. "I really wish I wasn't pregnant because I would slap the shit out of you," Sutton said giving Piper her attention again.

"I'm not about to listen to this bullshit, I gotta show to do." Saque waved them off, he knew that Sutton was about to spill the tea and he wasn't sticking around to listen. "Piper you can believe that shit if you want to but remember who's been there for you when she turned her back."

It was like Piper had a little devil and angel on her shoulder both telling her what to do at the same time, she was confused, and she hated it. She grabbed her head and shook it back and forth. Before she could respond her phone vibrated in her back pocket, she pulled it out and looked at it. She flipped through the pictures as tears rolled down her eyes.

"Really Saque? The bitch is pregnant and you out here like that's yo baby or some shit. I knew I shouldn't have trusted that hoe but you," she pointed at him with a face full of tears. "I can't believe that you would do me like that."

She turned the phone towards him and showed him the picture of him and Sunny hugged up at the lingerie shop. This particular picture was of him leaned over with his hands on her stomach while kissing on her neck. She was saying something about sucking his dick, he remembered because he licked her neck to demonstrate what he would do in return.

"Listen baby it wasn't what it looked like, I was in the mall and she approached me and asked me to go check out a few pieces with her and—"

"In a fucking lingerie store? You want me to believe you were helping the bitch shop?"

Piper belted it out, she was pissed beyond words. "Let me guess, she was helping you shop for me?" The hurt that flowed through her heart was unbearable. She turned her attention to Sutton she was ready to hand over a nice two piece to Piper's face. "Why now? Why tell me now Sutton so you could rub it in my face?"

Sutton stood back stunned at the words that were coming

out of her mouth. How could she even question her motives when she was just trying to be a good friend, something that Piper knew nothing about. She was sure that after this conversation, Piper would no longer exist to her.

"You have got to be fucking kidding me you stupid bitch." Sutton turned her head appalled at the situation at hand. She chuckled angrily before her eyes met Pipers. She took a few steps toward her, "I hope he dogs you the fuck out with that bitch. I want that nigga to give you hell and when everything around you begins to crumble remember who you turned your back on bitch."

"That's enough Sutton, let's go!" Kahleno pulled her to the back the minute he watched the first tear fall. He wasn't having her being upset and he made it his business to put out a word to figure out who the fuck this nigga was. He didn't know him but what he did know was if he ever spoke to or about Sutton like that again it would be the last person he ever spoke to.

~

Sunny saw everything go down and the minute that Sutton pointed at her she knew that she needed to dip until she could figure out a way to make this right. She headed to the back of the building where the stylist were preparing their models. Each salon was separated by a curtain making small rooms across the back of the room.

She dipped into the one that her and Piper were using to

prepare for the show to grab her things. She knew that Piper was going to be pissed if she found out that she was trying to get with Saque, and she wasn't in the mood or the position to handle that right now. It was like time wasn't on her side because the minute she came out of the makeshift room, Piper was waiting for her.

"I was there for you bitch when no one else wanted to fuck with you." Piper's face was full of tears. It felt as if someone was squeezing her heart in her chest. "Like I really want to know what the fuck is wrong with you, what ya pussy ain't good enough to get your own man? Huh hoe? You got to fuck with other people's men because you can't get your own?" with every tear that fell, Piper took a step towards Sunny quickly closing the gap that separated them.

"Now is not the time for this Piper," Saque growled pissed at the little scene that was unfolding before them and the attention that it had gained. It was the last thing that either of them needed, they were both building brands, and this definitely had the possibility to ruin that.

"Oh so I guess the proper time would have been when you were hugged up with this bitch in the fucking lingerie store?" Piper was hurt, she gave up her whole life for this man. She let him talk her into giving up her apartment and turning her back on her friend, now look. "Oh god Sutton was right." Piper covered her face with her hands and shook her head. "What did I do?"

"Baby, it's not like that I swear that was the only time I ever touched her." Saque said grabbing Piper and enclosing her in his arms. "I'm sorry I was just scared. I love you so much and that shit worries me. I'm so scared that you'll do what that bitch did." He spoke honestly, ever since he caught Key cheating on him it took every ounce of trust that he had left to give.

He watched his mother cheat on his father when he was younger, she would take him with her if his sisters were busy or she couldn't find anyone else to watch him. He grew a strong dislike for women at an early age and trusting them was out of the question. His father was a push over and he vowed to never be that kind of man.

He always kept his women close to him because when they were out of his sight, he knew that anything was game. Saque had a bad habit of needing to control his relationships to keep a tighter hold on his woman and that often ran them away or into the arms of another man. His love for Piper was getting too intense and he wanted to hurt her before she could hurt him kind of thing. Seeing the pain in her eyes made him feel like shit though and he knew he needed to make it right.

"Oh no I'm not going through that again." Sunny dropped her bag and walked closer. She was not about to be thrown under the bus like before. Saque was just as much of a participant in what they did as she was. "So you're saying that I flirted with myself, and that you didn't beg me to try this pregnant pussy." Sunny didn't care that she sounded like a whore she just wanted to make sure that she wasn't the only one getting the blame.

"You dirty bitch you threw yourself at me every chance

you got." Pipers breath got caught in her throat as Saque admitted to sleeping with Sunny. Flirting and rubbing against her was one thing but actually fucking her killed a small piece of Piper. She grabbed her chest and backed away. "Baby I'm sorry it was just one time and I regret it, every bit of it."

"No." Piper held her hands out for him to stop coming near her. "I'm done, I can't do this again." She cried and ran off. She couldn't believe that she was in this situation again. Her heart hurt and she could barely gather her thoughts. Right now she needed to get away from here and fast.

"Fuck!" Saque said as he tried to go after Piper but Sunny grabbed his arm. He looked down at her like she was crazy.

"Fuck her Saque, you got me. Let her go. I can run the beauty bar and we can be happy. I promise that you'll never regret choosing me." Sunny smiled like she had just won the lottery. She knew that Saque was her way out of the situation that she was currently in and she had to shoot her shot.

Saque never realized that Sunny was so desperate and thirsty until those words came out of her mouth. He never wanted to be with a woman like that and he couldn't explain why he even took it there with her.

Jerking his arm away he looked down to where Piper was quickly packing up her things so she could leave. Everyone that was in attendance was now standing outside of their little rooms watching the fireworks, including Sutton and the members of Chamber of Beauty.

"What I did with you was a mistake and you will never be anything other than what we are, which is nothing!" Saque spat making Sunny feel stupid as the smile on her face dissipated.

Her light skin turned bright red and the snickers from the audience that they had gained caused her stomach to roll. Here she was making herself look dumb for a man that belonged to someone else. She at least thought that she had a chance with Saque now here he was dissing her.

"You think she's gonna take you back?" Her voice trembled as tears threatened to fall but she didn't care. She already looked like an ass; she might as well get it all out. They were gonna talk about her anyway. The hair industry in Charlotte was small, she was sure that the *tea* had already made its way around the city.

"I don't give a fuck if she did or didn't that still don't mean I want you. You were something to boost my ego. That was fucked up because Piper didn't really deserve that from either of us." Saying the words out loud bothered him more than he thought they would.

He really did love Piper he just couldn't get the things that his mother and Akiya did to him out of his head and that pressed its way into his relationship with Piper. There was no one to blame but him and he knew that he was gone have to work overtime to fix it.

"Fuck you Saque, ya dick was whack anyway." Sunny said trying to save face but Saque shook his head.

"That's what's up, then it won't bother you that you won't get ya dick suckers around it again then." Saque shrugged his shoulders and took off in the direction of Piper.

"Ughhhhhh!" Sunny yelled and rubbed her stomach. She was feeling a little crampy, it was probably because she was on her feet all day. She looked around and when her eyes met Sutton's a coldness crept up her spine. Rolling her eyes she picked up her bags and stomped out of the event space.

When she got to her car, she broke down. Once again, her impulsive behavior had put her and her kids in a messed-up position. Saque used her, Piper was done with her, and she couldn't find Trouble. She was all alone, and she didn't know if she could deal with it.

Saque made his way into the room with Piper, she was slamming things around and throwing things every which way.

"Piper listen to me, don't do this. Regardless of how you feel right now you are here to do a job. Look at all your models. You need to bring business into your shop and acting off emotions is a bad move."

Piper stopped moving and sighed heavily, she knew that he was right, but she really didn't want to be anywhere near him right now. She had worked so hard to build the business just the way she liked it and she enjoyed being her own boss.

Sitting down in the chair she looked up at him. Every time her eyes blinked a tear rolled down her cheek and Saque felt more like an idiot. He finally had what he needed and had been looking for in Piper and this time he messed it up.

"Can you leave?" Piper turned to the table with the mirror attached. "I'll stay if you go to your room and leave me alone."

"Piper we have to talk about this."

"I really don't have anything to talk about. You did what you did, I feel how I feel, and it is what it is." She shrugged. On the outside she was trying to play it cool but, on the inside, she felt like her heart was about to rip out of her chest. "I just want to get through this show and then I'm gonna get my things and move out."

"What? Yo you bugging. I apologized for that shit and it won't ever happen again. You know what I been through and how that shit fucks with me. I messed up and I will do anything to make that shit up to you," Saque said damn near begging.

Piper wasn't perfect and there were a few things that she could work on, but he did love her and wanted to work things out with her. She was loyal and treated him like a king and he needed that desperately.

"What if it were me?" Piper asked.

"Huh?"

"I said what if it were me? What if I was the one that cheated on you? You would be ready to throw me to the wayside." She glanced at him through the mirror, but he had his eyes to the sky. He really didn't want to talk about this right now but there was no way around it. He was really hating Sutton right now. "I don't know why I keep doing this."

"Keep doing what?"

"Giving myself to niggas that don't deserve me." She shook her head. "The fucked-up part about it is Sutton tried to tell me a long time ago to be careful and slow down. Don't be so quick to fall in love, to figure out who you are first, and

I didn't listen. Now I'm sitting here feeling like someone knocked the wind out of me."

"Fuck Sutton she—"

"Don't you dare blame her!" Piper said sticking up for Sutton, something that she felt she should have done a long time ago. She hated that it took this long for her to realize that she was just looking out for her. Now she feels like it may be too late to apologize to her. Too much had been done. "She loves me."

"I love you."

"You gotta fucked up way of showing it," Piper said fixing her make-up.

"I know and again I'm sorry. I think we can get past this," Saque said confidently.

"I don't know if I want to get past this." Piper threw down her makeup brush. He would have to show her a lot for her to want to continue anything with him. Piper was starting to see things a little differently.

Saque walked in behind Piper and she looked at him through the mirror. He was trying to be patient with her because of the situation that he had put her in, but she was trying him. He placed his hands on her shoulders and lowered his lips to her ear so that only she could hear what he was about to say.

"If you want to keep the little life that you have you will, if you leave me, your leaving behind *A Touch of Beauty* by Piper," he said slowly, and her eyes stretched a little further with each word that he said. "I don't want to be like that, but I love you and I want us to get through this, if I have to use that to my advantage then so be it."

With that he walked off, leaving Piper with her thoughts. She had just gotten comfortable enough in her life to be happy about it. She was proud of her accomplishments and now she was left with choosing between her sanity and her livelihood.

~

"*N*o one's gonna fuck with you while I'm standing here." Cassidy boasted pissed off that Key was trying to leave.

She was scared out of her mind and didn't know what to do. Cassidy thought that she was scared of Saque because of what he did to her, but she was scared for a whole different reason. The last thing she needed was Saque questioning her about who Kane's father was.

"I'm good I swear I just need a minute," Key lied, she was trying to get the hell out of there before her secrets come out.

She didn't know how Cassidy would respond knowing that she kept a man from his kid. Key knew that it was selfish not telling Saque about Kane but the last thing she needed was to be tied to this man for eighteen years. She wanted to keep as much distance as she could between the two.

If Saque didn't know about him then it would make her life easier. Yes, it was selfish, and it ate at Key's conscious often, but she just couldn't subject herself to the torture of having to co-parent.

As if reading her mind, Cassidy grabbed her hands that were shaking, "Is there something that you need to tell me?" Cassidy tilted his head. He was starting to feel like her nervous energy was more than her seeing her ex.

"What, no," she shook her head and looked around for Kane. When she located him, she saw him and Kahlil chasing each other. They were at the side exit because she was trying to leave.

Her worst fear came true when Kane ran right into Saque and came tumbling down. Saque stopped in his tracks and looked down at the little boy that he had knocked down. Something felt familiar about him, his eyes and the way that they held a tint of light brown to them. The way his mouth curved down slightly.

"Aye ma, who this nigga?" Kane yelled out to his mother. "He look just like me."

Kane was very observant, sometimes too observant. He had a keen sense of knowing when something was wrong especially with his mother and when he looked back at her and he saw the tears streaming down her face.

"Whose son is he Akiya?" Saque asked as he glared at Key.

Cassidy stood back, looking back and forth between the two and he could feel his guard slowly making its way back up around his heart. He had asked Key on numerous occasions about who Kane's father was and she would always say that he wasn't involved. Never once did she say that he belonged to her ex and she had plenty of time to do so. He was definitely looking at her sideways.

"Let's go Kane," Key called out to her son who got up and ran to his mother who took his hand and started out of the building.

"The man asked you a question Key," Cassidy said grabbing her by her elbow to stop her stride. She jerked away from him and sucked her teeth.

"Who is and isn't my son's father is none of his fucking business and to be frank it isn't yours either." She hissed, not meaning to take her frustrations out on Cassidy but she couldn't help it. Right now she blamed him for not letting her leave when she wanted to.

"So we lying to each other now?" Cassidy slipped his hands in his pockets and took a step away from Key. He wasn't mad that her ex was her baby daddy, he was pissed that she felt she had to hide that from him, and she didn't have a reason to. That led him to believe that it was more to the story than what she was telling him.

"I didn't lie to you Cassidy."

"Omitting is lying."

"Is he my son?" Saque growled taking quick steps towards Key. He couldn't believe what he was saying. His head was spinning and pissed was an understatement. He was trying his best to remain calm, but this was too much. "Or does he belong to that other nigga or maybe he belongs to one of the niggas you were taking your clothes off for? I heard you were a good little prostitute." He didn't really hear that he was just heated and loved Key that much that he would say anything to help ease the confusion that was clouding his mind.

Cassidy glanced at Key who wore both a shocked and disgusted look on her face. She didn't think that he would take it there. When Saque went to jail and she found out she was pregnant with Kanaan she didn't know if it was Saque's or the guy she cheated with.

When she got him tested and it came back not his baby then she knew that Kane belonged to Saque. She was embarrassed to say the least to even have to question that. Saque was behind bars and his sister threw her out of the salon and blackballed her from working in another salon so she did somethings that she wasn't so proud of.

Webcam modeling is what paid the bills until Vinny started working for the Maler organization. She didn't get completely naked, but she did dance topless on the Webcam and got paid a hefty amount. She wasn't proud of it, but she didn't regret it either because raising a kid alone was expensive.

She never met any of her clients in person and she made sure to use an alias and cover her face. No one would ever know who she was unless they were able to identify her by the birthmark on her stomach. So what Saque was saying was a lie and he was doing it because Cassidy was standing there.

"You don't know what the fuck you're talking about," Key hissed as she pulled Kane along with her out the door. Cassidy went to follow her because he was taken aback by the comment made about her taking her clothes off for men, and possibly being pregnant by them. He was basically calling her a prostitute, at least that's the way that Cassidy took it and he didn't take her as that kind of woman.

"Is that my kid?"

"Leave me alone Saque, you've done enough." Saque tried to head in her direction but Cassidy stopped him. He was pissed at Key right now, but he wasn't about to let anyone hurt her. "Akiya!"

Key ignored him and put Kane in the car safely before getting in herself. Once she was in safely, she looked back over at Cassidy and the disappointed look on his face killed her. She was pissed that she was leaving him alone with Saque to fill his head with lies but she couldn't stay. She would just have to do damage control sometime tomorrow.

CHAPTER NINE

*C*rossing *Lines*

"Henny on the rocks and a Heineken," Cassidy said as he slid on the bar stool. His emotions were all over the place and he couldn't get them together. He just knew that Key was the woman that he needed in his life but the skeletons that were falling out of her closet bothered him.

Not only did she keep that man from his kid, but Saque pretty much called her a prostitute and she didn't deny it. Cassidy went back through his memory trying to think of a time when he got the inkling that she may be into something like that and he couldn't think of one time.

"Damn," Cassidy said to himself.

"Here you go handsome," the bartender slid his shot of Hennessy across the bar. She couldn't help but stare at the chocolate god that sat in front of her. From his tall frame to the broadness of his shoulders. Everything was sexy about this man, even the solemn look on his face.

Cassidy looked up and stared the bartender in her face. She was cute, her butterscotch colored skin was covered in strategically placed tattoos. They weren't too busy it was like each one of them had a purpose. She wore black booty shorts that fit her womanly curves. The sports bra that donned her upper half showed her wash board stomach.

The short haircut that she wore framed her slender face and brought out the lightness of her eyes. She was sexy but the only person on his mind was Key. He gave her a smirk and she could have sworn that she creamed her panties.

"Preciate that beautiful."

"Damn," she said as she watched his lips move. "Has anyone ever told you that you are sexy as hell?"

Cassidy chuckled at her bluntness. He loved a woman that was straightforward, it added to her sexiness. Dragging his tongue across his bottom lip he pulled it into his mouth and lightly bit down. He did it just to fuck with her and it was working, the sweat that formed on her brow let him know that.

"Keep on playing with me handsome and I'm gonna pull ya ass back here in the back and take you on the ride of your life. I won't even care about your girlfriend." She winked.

"Who said I got a girlfriend?"

"You did." She smiled and poured two shots of Hennessy, one for him and one for herself. "It's on the house." Cassidy lifted his glass and they toasted and took the shot.

"I never said anything, all I did was sit down and order a shot."

"I never said it was verbally." She leaned over on the bar allowing her breasts to spill out of the small top and gain Cassidy's attention. "I can tell by the way you walked in. Your shoulders were hunched and every step you took was heavy. The tone of your voice held hints of disappointment, like someone had let you down." She leaned in a little closer. "And when you looked at me the first time, your dick didn't get hard." She smiled wide causing one to spread on Cassidy's.

"So you read me like that huh?"

"Like a sexy ass, thick, orgasmic book." She tucked her bottom lip in between her teeth and lightly bit down while walking away to help another customer.

Cassidy's eyes followed her ass and he had to lick his lips at the way it moved inside of the tight black shorts that she wore. When she looked back at him, she winked making him shake his head.

"You just can't help yourself can you?" Cassidy grabbed the shot that he had originally ordered and took it to the head before turning to meet Piper's stare.

"What you talking about?" he asked pulling out his phone. He didn't want to talk to her right now. Giving advice to people who won't accept it wasn't on his list of things to do right now and he damn sure didn't want to talk about the situation with Saque and Key.

"The bartender, she wants to fuck you."

"Everybody wants to fuck me." Cassidy chuckled and then put his beer to his lips and turned it up.

"Everybody does not want to fuck you Cassidy," Piper slid on the stool next to him, big mistake. Cassidy leaned over and Piper immediately felt her nipples harden against the fabric of her bra.

"But you do," Cassidy turned so that he was facing her. "I can tell by the way your breathing sped up and your lip is sweating. You're trying your best not to look at me because you know that one look into my eyes and you're losing your panties. I won't even get started on the way your nipples are trying to stab their way out of that shirt." He licked his lips and bent down so that they were touching her ear. Every inch of cotton that lined the seat of her thong was soaking wet and she didn't even try to control that. "If I wanted to bend you over right now I could because I'm just that good."

Piper cleared her throat and leaned back from Cassidy. She grabbed the collar of her shirt and moved it back and forth to create some air. She was hot and he was right. If he wanted to fuck her tonight, she would be fair game.

"I'm gonna call you lucky, I would have paid for him to get that close to me." The bartender smiled looking at Piper. "What can I get for you sexy?"

"Can I get a *Surfer on Acid* please?" Piper said to the bartender who licked her lips and nodded her head.

"Have you ever tried a *Masturbating Butterfly*?" the bartender asked her, and she looked at Cassidy who looked back at the bartender with a smirk on his face.

"You a big ol' freak ain't you?" the bartender bent over laughing.

"Handsome and a sense of humor. Whoever she is, she's lucky as hell." She winked and then turned around to get what she needed to make the drinks. "But a *Masturbating Butterfly* is the same thing as a *Surfer on Acid,* you got Malibu Rum, Jager, and pineapple juice but you add Midori. You layer everything like this." She held the spoon upside down and slowly poured the pineapple juice first, then added the Malibu rum, followed by the Jager and then added just a small amount of Midori directly in the middle making the drink look like the wings of a butterfly.

"That shit is so pretty." Piper beamed as she reached for her glass. Pulling out her phone she snapped a picture of it and saved it to her Snap Chat. "That's dope." The bartender handed her the drink as well and then fixed Cassidy another shot while moving on to the other patrons.

The two sat in silence for a while, just milling over the events of the evening. Piper was still in her feelings about the whole Sunny and Saque thing, she felt so stupid, but she couldn't help who she fell in love with.

"Speak." Cassidy said. He felt her keep looking over at him like she wanted to say something, and he would rather her just say it.

"I don't know what I'm doing wrong." She said barely above a whisper. "Like this shit just keeps happening, I don't get it. I really thought Saque was the one for me."

"What's that nigga's parents name? What he like to do

besides fuck? Where was he born? Where's his family from? What makes him tick? What makes him happy besides pussy?" He looked at Piper while she lowered her head and nursed her drink. "Exactly, that's why it keeps happening. You don't take the time to get to know a nigga before you jump in the bed and fall in love."

"I bet you don't know anything about the Key bitch yet you fucking her." Envy dripped from Pipers lips.

"First of all watch your fucking mouth," Cassidy said through gritted teeth. He wasn't feeling her right now, but he wasn't about to sit and let Piper talk shit about her either. "You don't know shit about her. I on the other hand know that her mother's name was Diane and she died of cancer. I know that when she's nervous she chews on her bottom lip. She's silly as hell and if you can make her laugh than you win your way into her heart."

Cassidy sighed because even though he was saying all of this he didn't know if him and Key would even be a thing after what was said. That shit fucked him up about the taking her clothes off for money because he felt like that was something that she should have told him. Keeping shit like that away from him made Key look sneaky in his eyes. He knew that he would at least have to have a conversation with her but right now was not the time.

"You really like her, don't you?" Piper asked and Cassidy didn't answer. Truth was he really did but now he didn't know if he could trust her. "Umph! Did you know that Saque was her ex?"

"Nah I didn't, not that it would matter but I didn't know." Cassidy sipped on his beer. "The man didn't even know he had a son, there was no way that we would know anything." Cassidy chuckled.

"A son?" Piper whipped her head around.

"That's some shit you gone have to talk to him about, just like I need to holla at Key. I shouldn't even have said that shit. That was some bitch shit." Cassidy closed his eyes tightly hating that he even said anything about Kane possibly being Saque's.

"I don't even know if I want to find out anything else about him. I really want out, but I'm stuck."

"The fuck you mean you stuck Piper? If you don't want to fuck with that muthafucka no more then don't fuck with him. Simple as that." Cassidy glared at her. "He ain't holding no gun to your head making you stay, you staying because you want to stay."

"He paid for my shop." She said barely above a whisper. "I worked so hard for that and if I leave, he's gonna take it from me."

"Well then that's some bitch shit. No nigga should hold something that they done for you over your head, that's not a man." He could feel his anger rise because that's the same thing that Key said he did to her. "That's where you females mess up, let me ask you this... Is your name anywhere on the business?"

"Yeah, my name is on the building as a co-buyer and I have the LLC for *A Touch of Beauty* by Piper."

"Well then he can't take shit. The only thing that he can do is make you buy him out of his half of the loan for the building."

"But he bought all of the furniture and all of that. I'm sure he kept the receipts so when it all comes down to it, I will still be shit out of luck." Picking up her drink and chugging it she waved for the bartender to bring her another one.

"So you gone stay with this nigga, so you don't have to start over on your own?" He heard the words that were coming out of her mouth and he couldn't believe how superficial that some women could be. They would rather sell their souls than to make it happen on their own. That's the one thing that he could say about Key, she was independent, and he loved that.

"I love my business, Cassidy you just don't understand."

"But I do, I run a business. Actually my family has numerous businesses. Go to a bank and see what kind of loan you can get to buy him out and that way everything will be yours." What he was saying sounded simple to Cassidy, but it wasn't that simple for Piper because deep down she still loved Saque.

She thought that he was different, that he wouldn't do her like the other men did and for a while he didn't. He was the perfect gentlemen; he was invested in what she wanted out of life and he brought her vision to life. She was grateful but she didn't want to feel stupid in the process.

"He made me feel so comfortable and then played me like that." Piper confessed her true feelings, right before she put her head down. Cassidy didn't think there was any hope for Piper, but he couldn't deny that for some reason he had a little soft spot for her, so he tried to put her up on game.

"Because he could." She popped her head up, her eyes searched Cassidy's for understanding. It was something that she didn't know, and she felt like he had the answers. "You make it too easy. You don't make him work for nothing, the pussy, the loyalty, the heart, nothing. You met him and was like here nigga take this shit it's yours." Cassidy turned his beer up again. "I told you before if you don't know what you're worth no one else will care."

"I just want to be happy."

"But you ain't happy with yourself, so how do you plan to be happy with anyone else?" Cassidy glared at her while he waited for her to answer.

Piper pondered over what Cassidy was saying. Growing up she watched her mother get with these men and give them all of her just to get her rent paid. She watched as she catered to them for a new bag or bomb pair of heels. Not once did she ever witness her mother going out and getting it on her own. That was unheard of, her mother always told her that men were supposed to make ways and women were supposed to reap the benefits and that's what stuck with her.

Saque made the money and opened her up a business, he made a way for her to live how she felt she deserved to live. He did things to and for Piper that she would never think someone would do for her. Piper's mother use to always say, *"A lonely bitch is a broke one"*. Piper wanted to be neither.

"You have to make you happy shorty. If you ain't happy with you then you'll never be happy with anyone else. You be giving people too much control over your life and that's where you fuck up." Cassidy turned so that he was facing her. "When muthafuckas get that much control they use that shit to the best of their ability, and you end up disappointed." Cassidy lifted Pipers chin so that she was looking at him. "Let me ask you this...do you love that nigga?" Piper nodded her head. "Okay, why?"

She took a minute to think about what she wanted to say before she said it. Cassidy made her nervous when he talked to her like this, but she also knew that she needed it. He had a way of putting things into perspective for her even if she didn't listen.

"He helped me get on my feet. When me and Sutton fell out, he was there to make sure that I got clients, so I didn't lose out on money. I've always wanted my own beauty bar and he made that happen. I have access to his accounts, and he makes sure that I stay fly. I've never had a man take care of me like he does."

"But at what cost?" Cassidy shook his head. She was more superficial than he thought. "Not once did you say because the way he makes you feel. Like how when y'all are together, nothing else matters. Or what about the way he brings out the best in you. Everything you said was surface, and superficial as fuck. You need to grow up beautiful." Cassidy called for another shot.

Piper looked at him and nodded her head. What he said

was true and she knew it. The two sat at the bar and talked until the bar closed. When it was time to go, Piper didn't want to go home and face Saque, and Cassidy was enjoying her company. He invited her to come sleep on his couch or in his spare room and she agreed.

~

*K*nock! *Knock! Knock!* The banging on the door woke Piper up from her drunken stupor. She opened her eyes and the minute she did the room began to spin and she shut them tight again. She couldn't remember anything that happened after her and Cassidy left the bar. She remembered the conversation getting a little lighter and they started to have fun.

The drinks were coming like water, it was like as the night went on the bartender made them a little stronger. With everything going on she felt like she needed to have a night like that. She definitely appreciated him for it.

Knock! Knock! Knock! The person on the other side of the door wasn't letting up and as bad as she wanted to ignore it, she couldn't. Pulling herself up to the sitting position she slowly opened her eyes and looked around. She was in a living room, one that didn't belong to her.

Grabbing her head she tried her best to remember where she ended up the night before but to no such luck. Standing to her feet she struggled to the door as she pulled it open and came face to face with the girl Key, the one that was with her ex.

"Oh yeah?" Key said with much distain. She didn't hold back the ill feelings that she felt seeing the woman that was with her ex now standing at the door of the man that she called herself falling for.

"You looking for Cassidy?" Piper said still not fully functioning. Her mind was on her splitting headache and not the woman standing in front of her with a very displeasing scowl.

When she finally focused, she realized who the woman was. Piper could have easily told her what was up because from the look on her face she thought that her and Cassidy did something. She opened her mouth to say something then she remembered that this woman was the reason that she was in the situation that she was in with her man. She was the reason that Saque didn't trust so she didn't feel like she owed her shit.

"Nah." Key released an angry chuckle before she slowly started to back away. "No thanks, I think I actually found the real him." She smiled and then jogged to her car.

Key was trying to tell herself that she wasn't hurt by this revelation, but she was. Even though her and Cassidy hadn't been physical but a few times, they had been talking and getting to know each other longer.

She knew for a fact that she wanted to be more than just friends and he said that he did to. The two agreed to take their time but Key didn't know that take their time meant sleeping with other people. Staring back at Cassidy's door watching as it closed, she felt like her heart was closing too, closing to the thought of them being together.

Cassidy was pissed last night, she could see it in his eyes but what Saque said wasn't completely true and she felt like she owed him an explanation, which was why she was here. Now she didn't think he deserved a second thought when it came to her.

Pulling out of the driveway she headed to the shop, she had a few appointments and she needed something to get her mind off of what she just saw. Lines had been crossed and she didn't know if they would ever be the same.

CHAPTER TEN

Tell Me
Chills ran up and down Icelynn's spine as AD moved in and out of her. She arched her back to give him the access he requested, and it proved to be rewarding when he tapped her g-spot a few times before he slid out and entered her again.

"I fucking love you, you know that?" AD sunk his teeth into his bottom lip. His hands caressed the meatiness of her cheeks as he had his way with her.

"I love you too," flowed from her lips effortlessly.

The words they spoke were nothing but the truth. Everything had lined up for them lately and they couldn't be happier. AD had hired Icelynn as the manager of the restaurant and they were due for the grand opening soon. They both were excited surprisingly.

"Say that shit again Ice."

"Ummm shit baby right there." She started throwing her ass back on him. "Fuck I love you baby."

"Shit Ice, take that shit then." He thrust into her as he watched her throw her ass back, wrapping her pussy muscles around his dick. His orgasm was on the rise and he knew it. "You gone make me nut."

"Come with me baby." She cried out. "Oh God." The hairs on the back of her neck stood up as a shiver worked its way from her pussy to her shoulders. Her stomach knotted up as the most powerful orgasm shot through her. "Yes baby!" she cried out.

"Fuck Ice!" AD cried out as he released everything that he had into her waiting womb. Icelynn fell face forward and AD fell beside her. They both were breathing hard and trying to catch their breath from the powerful session they had engaged in.

AD looked up at the ceiling, thinking back to everything that he had been through the last few months. He couldn't believe that all that shit had transpired. It was enough to drive him insane but thanks to Icelynn and Dr. Reems he seemed to be doing a little better.

The two had actually just came from seeing Dr. Reems and she encouraged AD to tell his family what happened to him when he was younger. He was a little apprehensive, but he knew that it was something that he needed to do.

Isis was doing so much better too, she still had night-mares every once in a while, but she was more comfortable being in crowded spaces. Sometimes they had family sessions and sometimes Isis went alone so she could speak freely. All and all they were all getting over the things that held them back.

"I gotta go meet these fools at the hospital, I guess Ma up there showing her ass cause she ready to come home even though they want her to stay a little longer." He chuckled but Icelynn was quiet. He leaned up and looked over at her. "What's up baby?"

"Did you mean it?" her eyes danced around his while she waited for an answer. "When you said I love you did you mean it?"

"More than anything girl." He climbed back on top of her and leaned down and crashed his lips against hers. "I don't think I can live without you and Isis. Y'all got me through one of the toughest times of my life and I will never be able to thank you enough, so I'll prove it every day of my life. I'm ready to spend forever with you."

Tears formed in her eyes as she felt every word that came out of his mouth. She didn't have to question it anymore, she knew, and she felt the same. Easing back in her AD slowly made love to his woman until he felt like there was no doubt left in her mind.

~

"Why you in here making all that noise ol' lady?" AD said when he walked in the room with his family. Everyone was there and Siya was up fussing at all of them because they wouldn't take her home.

"Where the hell you been? You were supposed to be here three hours ago," Siya fussed the minute her baby boy was in her face.

She had been stuck in the hospital for over two weeks now and she was pissed about it. Her health was improving daily, and she could hold a conversation without coughing. Her arm was healing, she had even started physical therapy for her leg. She could do all of that at home, and that's where she wanted to be.

"Me and Icelynn had therapy earlier today."

"Okay that was earlier, you said that you were on your way three hours ago," Siya pried. AD smirked and pulled out his phone and took a seat in the chair by her bed.

"I was making you another grandbaby." He simply said making his brother and father laugh.

Siya smacked her lips because she knew that AD was only joking although she would love it if he did have a baby by Icelynn, she thought she was good for him. All of her boys were in successful relationships, all except for Cassidy which she had just got done fussing at.

"Whatever come here Adoreé." She said and motioned for him to come closer to her. They hadn't really talked since she told him what happened with Ziva and she needed to know how he felt about it because it wasn't something that she just wanted to slide under the rug. "I know the last time we really talked I laid some heavy stuff on you and I want to make sure you were okay."

"Yeah Ma I'm good, I never felt a connection to her. Like when I met with her all I felt was the need to slit her throat. There was nothing there, so I knew something was off." AD shrugged his shoulders and sighed. "I really don't care about anything other than the fact that you are my mother, you raised me and that's good enough for me."

Tears fell from Siya's eyes, "Do you forgive me?" she asked him through her tears.

"Of course ma, stop all that crying. I thought you were a G?" AD joked and Siya slapped him in the head. "But I won't feel better until that bitch is dead." The coldness of his tone when he said that slithered its way into Siya's heart. She knew the men in her life were out for blood and she wasn't going to hold them back because Ziva's head on a platter would more than satisfy her.

"I'm glad you've been going to counseling and I'm sorry all of this made you feel like you need to. I feel horrible about all of it." Siya wiped the tears that were rolling down her face.

AD knew that it was now or never and even though he didn't want to relive this situation again he knew in order for him to heal he needed to tell the people that he loved the most. Staring in the eyes of his family he was kicking himself for not letting Icelynn come with him.

She had done enough for him and she deserved a little time with her friends, and he wasn't going to hold her back from that.

"That's not the sole reason for me going to therapy ma." He cleared his throat.

"Well why are you going? Adoreé tell me."

AD took a deep breath as he rehashed the horrible things that he had to endure when he was a child. He told them everything, ever act, every feeling, he didn't leave not one stone unturned and when he was done every man in the room had a stone face and Siya was sobbing crying.

This was the first time that AD had talked about the traumatic event and not shed a tear and it felt good. That meant he was in the beginning stages of the healing process. Most black people didn't believe in therapists and for a while he didn't either, but he was thankful that Icelynn talked him into it.

"You should have told me," Mega's voice boomed in the room. He was so pissed that his son went through that alone. Even though he killed the sick bastard, he could have been there through that with him.

"I couldn't." AD shook his head. "I was ashamed, I was a boy. I felt like I should have fought harder. That maybe if I would have stood my ground it wouldn't have happened. I blamed myself for a long time. That shit ate at me every day, but I just couldn't tell you, I wanted to, but the words would never come out."

Siya didn't know if there was an explanation for her feelings, but she couldn't escape them. She wished that she could have taken that pain away from him, she hated that he had to live with that.

"You killed that nigga like that," Cassidy said as he got up and walked over to his brother. He dapped him up and pulled him out of his seat into a brotherly hug. "I wish you would have told me I would have slit his fucking throat, and Senior too for being related to his bitch ass. I love you nigga." They patted each other on the back.

Kahleno followed suit and then they all stood around Siya's bed who wasn't saying anything. She was thinking back to the attempted murder charge he almost caught when he was younger.

"When you got in that fight at the basketball court, when you beat that little boy up and you told us you were fighting for Menz. Did he know?"

"Ion no, I guess Menz must have said something about that nigga fucking with him. So we were playing ball and that nigga said something about Menz being gay and shit because his uncle was fucking him." AD slipped his hands into his pockets nervously. "Then the nigga turned to me and said it must be me fucking his uncle too and I spazzed. I tried to break every bone in his face."

"I know nigga I had to pay a hefty amount to make that shit go away." Mega shook his head and then stood to hug his son. "I hate you had to deal with that shit on your own, makes me feel like I was less than a man because I couldn't protect my son."

"Don't do that, I didn't tell you and that was my choice. I should have and I see that now but what's done is done." He shrugged his shoulders.

Mega nodded his head and then took a seat back in his chair. He was not only frustrated by the news that his son had just revealed but he had been having a hard time finding Ziva. When Marlin came, he told him that Ziva tried to get him to help her kill Siya, but he refused.

"What's up Pops?" Kahleno said noticing the change in Mega's demeanor. Mega smirked at his son and straightened himself up in his seat.

"When I first brought your mom here, Marlin showed up." Cassidy bit down on his back teeth and Kahleno sat up in his chair to wait for his father to continue. "He let me know that he was there to warn me. Ziva asked him to help her kill your mother but he declined because of his respect and business relationship with me."

"I find it funny that he waits until some bullshit happens to come and *warn* you." Cassidy was skeptical of Marlin, but he didn't trust anyone so Mega knew that was coming.

"At the end of the day that's still his family, I think he was more so trying to stay out of it but when she fucked with him it became a different story. I respect that."

"What you mean, fucked with him?" Kahleno asked.

"She burned the cocoa farm, over one hundred fifty million dollars gone." Mega swiped his hand across his throat emphasizing what he was saying. "I don't know what that means for us, right now you're good right?" He looked at AD because he was closer to the street dealings than the other two were.

"I need to check with Spiff, I don't know for sure, but shit been moving since we got rid of the weak links. So we might be looking soon."

They only got a shipment once a month, they got so much at one time that that's all that they needed. With the pills and weed they had a steady flow with the drug side of the Maler empire.

"Do that and let me know, I'm supposed to meet with Marlin later to see where he's at with finding this bitch." Mega growled.

"Got damn what is she a ghost?" Cassidy said truly confused. It was like this woman kept getting close to them and now no one could find her.

"Nah but she's good at disappearing, when you've been in the game long as we have you learn certain skills and disappearing is one of them." Mega sat back in his seat. Shaking his head he needed to get a handle on Ziva if he ever wanted to live comfortably.

They talked a little while longer and then they all got up to leave. Mega told Siya that he was going to walk them out. She fussed about giving them two days to get her out of here or she was breaking out herself.

"Cassidy hang back for a second," Siya said as they all filed out the door. Cassidy sighed and rolled his eyes because he knew what she wanted to talk about. "Roll 'em again and I'ma knock 'em out Cassidy Maler."

"What's up ma?" he said with a smirk on his face.

Siya took in the smug look on her son's face and couldn't help but to shake her head. Cassidy had always been the most straightforward out of her three boys. He didn't hold back what he thought or how he felt. So the way he was treating Key was confusing to her.

"Don't what's up me, I talked to Akiya the other day when she came up here with Sutton and Icelynn."

"Why she even come up here, we don't rock like that no more." He said smoothly.

"And why not? Did you even have a conversation with her?" Siya fussed.

That morning when Cassidy woke up, he was home alone, thank goodness. He was so drunk the night before that he feared that he'd done something that he would later regret. Even though he had a soft spot for Piper, he knew that she wasn't someone that he would settle down with.

She was too immature for him. He also knew that she had been through enough of men using her and even if she didn't respect herself, he respected her enough for the both of them.

"Ma I just don't like how she moving. I don't need that shit in my life. If I have to second guess everything you tell me then I don't want nothing to do with you to be honest." He shrugged his shoulders.

"You think she's perfect and she's not. That's why you've never settled down because you've been looking for the perfect woman and you are never gonna find her. She doesn't exist son." Siya reached for her son's hand.

"I never said my girl had to be perfect, but I want her to have some got damn morals. She kept that boy from that man on purpose. I know he took her through hell, but that man still deserved to know he had a kid out there." Cassidy hated that Key wasn't who he thought she was because he could have really saw himself with her in the long run.

"Do you know the story?"

"She told me that he tried to kill her and how he stopped her money flow when he got locked up. I get that, but not telling that man he had a kid was selfish as fuck." Cassidy looked at his mother for validation for what he was feeling. "Say she got pregnant with my kid and I pissed her off. Who says that she won't run off and keep some shit like that from me? That shit is hard to trust."

"She only did what she thought was best for herself and her son. Yeah not telling him may have held some selfish intentions but that was her decision and she's learned from it." Siya squeezed Cassidy's hand. "You can't judge her situation if you didn't live it."

"I'm not judging her I just—"

"You're just judging her. She may have been scared for her life or her child's life. You don't know that because you're stubborn ass didn't have a conversation with her." She slapped his hand. "You need to have a conversation with her if it's not too late."

"What you mean if it ain't too late?"

"Oh Piper didn't tell you?" Siya lowered her eyes at her son.

"Tell me what?"

"Akiya came to see you the morning after all of that

happened at the hair show and Ms. Piper opened the door for her." Siya smirked.

"That's why I ain't heard from her, I thought she was staying away because she was guilty as fuck but..." Cassidy threw himself back in the chair as he let everything that his mother said roll through his mind. "Fuck!"

Cassidy was so wrapped up in wanting a woman with no flaws that he forgot to embrace the good in her. He let his perception of what he thought a woman should be cloud his judgment and push away the woman that was meant for him. He could admit it to himself that he had fucked up, he just hoped it wasn't too late to fix it.

"I take it you're going to apologize and talk to her?" he nodded his head. "Listen when she talks if she'll even talk to you. You may not agree with what she's saying, you may not even like it, but she did what was best for her and her kid. You always told me that you wanted a woman that was head strong and made her own way. Well that's Akiya and she's not about to let you or anyone else let her feel bad about her decisions. And I don't blame her." Siya closed her eyes and laid her head back on the pillow.

"Yes ma'am." Cassidy laughed because he knew when his mother closed her eyes that she was done with the conversation. He stood up prepared to go and talk to Key.

CHAPTER ELEVEN

*C*onversations

"I can't believe that you still ain't talk to him," Sutton said placing a fry in her mouth.

Key told her all about what went down with them at the hair show, even about Piper's man Saque being her ex. When she divulged that information the argument that him and Sutton had become more clear.

"Hey y'all, chill out." Icelynn looked at the table across from them where the kids were sitting. They were throwing fries at each other and getting riled up.

"Nope and honestly I don't want to. Like he literally played me to the left for that bitch. Never even gave me a chance to explain. I swore to myself that I would never let a man do that to me again." Key took a deep breath; she could feel herself getting worked up.

"I can't believe Piper even got the chance to be in the same room with Cassidy. When we met them, she was fucking with his cousin Menz. Cassidy had to break up a fight between him and her. Cassidy ain't the type of nigga that go for girls like that." Sutton attempted to play devil's advocate.

"Well clearly he's a lot of things he says he's not." Key grabbed her chicken sandwich and took a bite out of it. "I'm good though."

"No you ain't you miss him, I can see it on your face," Icelynn said knowing that look oh too well. She felt the same way when AD up and dipped on her. It was something about those Maler men that just drew you in and held you.

"I miss him like crazy but he ain't about to play me and I put that on my son."

"Speaking of, have you heard from Saque? I'm surprised he ain't tried to reach out." Sutton asked.

"He saw my brother on the block and tried to approach him and Vinny crazy ass tried to shoot him," Key laughed. "I don't know why he would even try and approach my brother knowing he didn't like him like that. Vinny hated Saque because he was controlling, and he used money to try and control people. He buys you anything you want; even helps you build your dreams but the minute you do something he don't like then he snatches it from up under you."

"I bet that's how Piper got that beauty bar," Icelynn interjected.

"I guarantee it," Key said raising her eyebrows. "Man, I couldn't even go to the gym without him calling me at least four times, then when I would get back home it was a fight because he wondered who I was talking to while I was there."

"Oh hell no, I would have cheated too," Sutton said causing them all to laugh.

"Girl the minute I got an out I jumped on it. *Literally.*" They all laughed again. "I feel bad about getting ol' boy involved though he didn't deserve that."

"Girl that wasn't on you that was on that crazy—" Sutton's words trailed off as the man of the hour walked right into a conversation about him.

Saque glared at Sutton. He was pissed at her because Piper was still pissed at him. She had finally come home but she wasn't talking to him and it was all because of her. When his attention diverted to the kids' table he began to walk in their direction.

Key hurriedly jumped up and stopped him from approaching her son. They were not about to do things like this. She knew that she was going to have to have a conversation with him, but he was not about to approach her son like they knew each other.

Kane was not dumb, he knew that something was going on with the strange man that looked like him and his mother, he was just waiting on his mother to talk to him about it. He also knew that the strange man that looked like him was also the reason that Cassidy hadn't been back around.

"He's my son, I got a right to see him."

"No the fuck you don't." Key stood in front of him. Her demeanor was definitely confrontational because she wanted him to know that he didn't run anything when it came to her or Kane, so he could either play by her rules or don't play at all.

"How the fuck could keep some shit like that to yourself? That's bullshit Akiya and you know it." Saque was fuming, the little boy looked to be about five or six and he didn't know a thing about him. Not even his name.

"You tried to fucking kill me Saque. Like you shot at me and if wasn't for ol' boy jumping in front of the bullet, me or Kanaan wouldn't be here right now." She fussed with tears in her eyes.

"I gave you the world and you cheated on me." He stepped in her face and the emotions that he felt the day he caught her came rushing back. All he could see was the look on his father's face when he caught their mother, his father cried and went in the living room until she finished. His father was weak, he never wanted that to be him and he proved that it would never be.

"No you dangled the world in my face so I would do whatever you said. You suffocated me, I couldn't breathe while I was in a relationship with you, can't you see that? You so ready to blame everyone for your problems but you can't see the part that you play in your drama!" Key yelled louder than she intended to. "You didn't love me, you just wanted to control me, and I couldn't take it anymore. I should have just left but you made it hard for me. I'm sorry for cheating but I needed to be free."

"You think any of that changes the fact that you held my son from me?"

"It doesn't have to change a thing Saque and I'm sure that you will never change either, which is another reason why I kept Kane a secret. Over my dead body will he ever act like you, ever!" she pointed in his face.

"I just want to meet my son." He slapped her hand down and Kane jumped up and pushed him.

"Put yo hands on my mama again punk!" he boasted.

"Yeah make us whoop yo ass!" Kahlil joined in.

"We'll fork you up!" Isis joined the crew twirling a fork in her hand with a sinister smile on her face.

"Alright kids, I'm okay, go back and sit down. We're about to go in a minute," Key tried to get the kids to move but they didn't budge.

"Hey little man, my name is Saque and I'm your..."

"No!" Key yelled and pushed Saque back. "Go sit down right now Kane." She pointed to the table.

She grabbed Saque by the arm and pulled him along with her outside. They had caused enough of a scene. She could see the waitress wanting to tell her that they had to leave but the sympathetic look in her eyes wouldn't let her.

"Get yo fucking hands off of me Akiya." He snatched away from her right as they hit the door. "You can't keep me from him. I'll go to court and get full custody if you fuck with me."

"Oh yeah tell me what fucking court gone give full custody to a nigga that ain't too long got out of jail from attempted murder!" she yelled in his face and he backed down because he knew it was true. There was no way that he would ever get custody of his son because of his past. He hated that he didn't have control over this situation but right now he didn't have any cards to play, he was at her mercy.

"I just want to get to know my son, all that shit in the past, it's whatever. I just want to know Keem?" he asked her, and Key softened her expression.

As much as she hated him, she knew it was wrong to keep Kane from him all this time. For the sake of her son she would at least try to allow him to get to know him, but it would be up to Saque how long it lasted because the minute he tried to start his shit she was gone cut that shit short.

It was a big step for her to even be having this conversation with him. She knew that she couldn't allow the hate that boiled in her heart for him to overshadow her son's needs. Even after everything that he put her through after he was locked up, it made her who she was. They both did some messed up stuff and it took seeing his face for her to realize that.

"His name is Kanaan. Kanaan Lamar Delaney, I call him Kane for short." She searched his eyes for some sort of reaction but there wasn't one. "WE can set up a time for you to take a DNA test if you want to and then from there, we can figure out a way to introduce you to Kane."

"DNA test? Got damn, how many niggas you cheat with?" he narrowed his eyes at her, and she rolled hers.

"Just one, but I've already had him tested and he's not Kane's father."

"I bet you wish his was, don't you?"

"Yep! I sure the hell did, but here we are." Key shrugged, she wasn't about to let him make her feel bad about for something she did years ago, and she had already apologized for. "WE gone do things my way or no way, I've raised him for the last five, six years. His birthday is next month."

"That was by choice."

"You were in jail, what were you gonna do? Throw the football with him through the glass?" Key sassed and then threw her hands up, she didn't want to argue with him. "Look I don't want to argue, what's done is done and we have a son. We've both made mistakes, so let's correct them now."

The solemn look in his eyes made Key regret keeping him away but there was nothing that she could do about it now. They could only move forward, her feelings towards him hadn't changed but she couldn't continue to be selfish when it came to Kane. He deserved to know who his father was, she just hoped she was making the right decision.

"Me being in jail doesn't excuse you from keeping my son from me, that's just wrong but I'm willing to put that behind me if you give me a chance to be in his life," Saque said and Key nodded her head.

"Do you need a DNA?" she asked because she was willing to get one.

"Yeah, I don't really trust you so I would just rather get one to be on the safe side." Saque threw out there to try and keep the upper hand. Key shook her head and went to walk off. "So when can I see him?"

"After the DNA comes back." She winked and threw up her deuces.

He wanted to be smart then she could too. There was no way that she was going to allow him to run her life. She may have had to be tied to him, now that he knew about Kane, but it was gonna be on her terms.

Walking back into the restaurant Key smiled at her growth, she was scared that it would backfire in her face, but she knew she had to do what was best for her son. When she sat back down the girls looked at her.

"Sooooo!"

"We had it out, but I told him that after the DNA test came back that we could talk about Kane." She shrugged. "As bad as I don't want anything to do with him, I know that Kane could benefit from having his father in his life." She looked over a Kane. "I just hope I'm not making a huge mistake."

~

*P*iper was in the spare bedroom folding clothes, that's where she had been since she came home from Cassidy's house. She didn't tell him that Key stopped by, it slipped her mind and after she got herself together, she called an Uber and left and hadn't talked to him since.

The house that she once called a home was a mess, Saque was walking around apologizing like that was supposed to solve everything but it solved nothing. She was hurt and she needed him to acknowledge that.

Bam! The front door slammed, indicating that Saque was home from work. She looked at the time on her apple watch and realized that he was home early. Normally he would find where she was and go on and on about how he missed her, but he never made it past the living room.

"Saque?" Piper called out to make sure that it was him that came into the house. When she didn't get an answer, she hurriedly picked up her phone to call him. Her heart was beating out of control and her hands began to get moist. She was scared.

She heard his phone ringing in the living room she shut her phone off and headed in this direction. His head was thrown back against the couch and his arms were over his eyes, the conversation that he had with Key played over and over in his mind.

"Am I a bad person Piper." He asked her without moving his arms. "Like do I make you hate me?" his tone lacked confidence, sounding as if he was trying to find himself.

"No what you did is making me hate you," Piper answered unaware of the underlining reason for the conversation at hand.

"When I was younger," he took a deep breath to prepare himself to open up to this woman whom he had deep feelings for. "My mother used to take me with her to cheat on my dad." He finally moved his hands from his face and looked up at Piper who wore a shocked expression. "My father was weak, and he loved my mom so much that the thought of her leaving him outweighed the disrespect that she showed."

"Oh no I'm so sorry." Piper walked around and eased her way into his lap.

"I always told myself that I would never be like him, so it's like whenever I get close to a woman and I start to love her I get scared." He shook his head. "I made Akiya hate me to the point she kept my son away from me. I've gotta son, he'll be six years old next month and I just learned his name today. You know how that fucks with me."

"You don't know how to let people in, you have to stop thinking that every woman is your mother."

"But Key cheated on me."

"I don't condone cheating in no shape or form, and we will talk about that in a minute, but you have to ask yourself what part did you play in it. Why did she feel the need to go to someone else?" Piper searched his eyes for an answer.

"She said that I smothered her and tried to control her life," he groaned. "Do you feel that way?"

"I do!" Piper answered honestly. "You cheated on me, you did the one thing that you are afraid of and then you threatened me with my business if I left you because you made a mistake. What sense does that make?" Piper tilted her head. "Sometimes you treat me like I'm your property instead of your woman, but I never required you to do otherwise."

The words that Cassidy spoke to her that night at the bar resonated through her mind. She smiled at the thought of his voice telling her that she needed to know what she was worth before anyone else would care. It hurt to hear some of the things that he told her, but she had to admit, she listened to everything that he said.

"What do you mean?"

"Meaning, I'm so eager to be in love and in a relationship that I allowed you to do and talk to me any kind of way. I took the things that you did for me as love and that's not love." She ran her hand down the side of this face.

"So you're saying that I was your bank and that you don't love me."

"What I'm saying is that I don't even love myself," she said honestly. "I really care about you, like when I found out that you were fucking Sunny it damn near killed me and that had nothing to do with superficial things. It had everything to do with my heart."

After her conversation with Cassidy she had a little while to think about what she needed and what was in her heart. Even though she measured Saque's love for her through monetary gain she knew that she still felt something for him. She was genuinely hurt by the fact that they may not be together anymore.

"What do you need from me?" Saque asked surprising Piper.

"I need you to take a step back, and let me figure out who I am." Her eyes bore into his. The sad look that took over his face made her heart flutter; she knew that he cared in that moment she felt it in her heart. "While we really get to know each other."

"So you forgive me?"

"This time but if it happens again, then I'm out."

"I promise you won't ever have to worry about that again, I know better." Saque smiled.

"There are a few more things that we need to talk about too, but we can get to that later." He nodded. "Ohhhh and I want my name on the building too. I worked hard for that and I deserve it." He looked at her skeptically. "I don't want you trying to use that against me ever again that shit tore my soul."

"I'm good on that Piper. I know I got shit to work out about my family but I'm off that dumb shit. I want to get to know my son and I know I got to get my head together before I can do that."

"And I get that baby, but I need you to show me," Piper said. "Add my name to the building," she said and Saque playfully rolled his eyes.

"Aight damn!"

"Oh and Sunny is fired, if I see her anywhere near my establishment, I'm gone forget she's pregnant. That bitch is foul, and I'm done with her, no second chances. And if I even think you communicating with her, I'm going off." Piper pointed at him.

"What else baby?" Saque knew that he had a long way to go but he was gone try his best.

"Nothing, now tell me about your son." She listened while Saque told her what little he did know. He told her how he wanted to meet him, but Key was making him wait until after the test came back.

"It's crazy that I haven't even had a conversation with the kid yet and I love him already. Like I'm ready to change my whole life around for him." Saque stared off.

"Well I'm right here for you." Piper kissed his cheek and then his lips. The kiss went from sensual to nasty in a matter of minutes and the two spent the rest of the day exploring each other and making up for lost time.

CHAPTER TWELVE

*Y*our Turn

"Stop Kahleno," Sutton whined as Kahleno subtly licked her nipples that were standing at attention and begging for attention.

"Well I suggest you put them up if you don't want them in my mouth." Kahleno chuckled as he trailed his tongue around her supple mounds. The pregnancy had made her breasts more round and Kahleno couldn't get enough.

Sutton's breathing picked up as she began to arch her back feeding him more of her. He began to flick his tongue over her nipple in a teasing manner taking her over the edge. Soft moans left her lips as she grabbed the back of his head pulling him into her.

"Baby, shit," she moaned out breathily.

"I thought you wanted me to stop." A smirk slowly spread

across his face as he slowly kissed each breast then traveled down the center of her torso stopping at her belly button. Sutton giggled as he took a dip into it.

"Stop teasing me." Kahleno looked up into her eyes and they told him a story that he couldn't wait to hear.

Spreading her legs enough to expose her clit he quickly flicked over it causing her to gasp at his touch. He moved his tongue slow and sensual around it until it back hard and her soft moan became more audible, the way he liked them.

With his hand on the inside of her thigh he inched it over to where his thumb danced around her opening creating an intense surge of electricity to flow through her body. She shivered as his thumb purged broke through the barrier and instantly became soaked in her juices.

"Got damn," Kahleno said against her clit and the vibrations alone drove her crazy. She clawed at the back of his head as she buried his face into her and began sucking like his life depended on it.

"Oh baby, oh Kahleno yes." Sutton arched her back and grabbed her breast and rolled her nipples around with her thumb and middle finger. This pregnancy had her hormones at an all-time high, so it wouldn't take long to give in to the explosive orgasm that was on its way.

Ding dong! Ding dong!

The doorbell sounded making Kahleno lift his head from Sutton's greatness. She looked down at him like he had lost his mind. She was on the brink of a mind-blowing orgasm and him stopping was not an option. Grabbing the back of his head to push him back into her, Kahleno chuckled and shook his head lose from her grasp.

"Who the fuck is that?"

"I don't really care; you need to finish this," she whined lazily. Her body had prepared her for what was to come and there was no way that he could leave her unsatisfied. He had never done it before, and he wasn't gonna start now.

"You just gone leave whoever it is outside?"

"If it's important they will wait." She grabbed his head and pushed it back in between her legs. Kahleno was more than skilled when it came to pleasing her, whether it be with his mouth or that magic stick that he was blessed with and every time they made love it was that much more special to her. "Come on baby I was... Ummmm," she moaned when he covered her pussy with his mouth and sucked gently. "Yesss daddy," she cried out.

Kahleno's thick tongue moved across Sutton's swollen clit before it wrapped around and was taken into his mouth. He sucked gently while inserting two fingers into her tight wet tunnel. He knew how to get her to where she needed to be.

"Yes baby that's it, oh shit." She screamed as her orgasm hit the pit of her stomach and rumbled there for a minute before it shot electric currents throughout her body causing her to shake. "Oh god I'm coming."

Ding dong! Ding dong! Ding dong!

Whoever was outside wasn't letting up, but Sutton wasn't allowing them to take her from her high. She ignored the sound of the doorbell and the sound of their ringing phones.

Kahleno on the other hand was on high alert. With everything that had been going on, someone that persistent made him feel like something was wrong.

Taking back possession of his drenched fingers he stuck both of them in his mouth and sucked her juices off of them. She looked up at him with a lazy smile. While Kahleno took off in the direction of the bathroom she contemplated which way she was going to turn to try and get comfortable so she could take her a nap.

"Oh shit that's your dad," Kahleno said with humor in his tone. "Get yo ass up."

"Noooo tell him I'm sleep, I'm so tired Kahleno."

"Didn't nobody tell your nasty ass to do all of that. I done told yo ass about that shit anyway. Don't be grabbing my head, I know what I'm doing," Kahleno fussed while Sutton released a subtle giggle. He hated when she grabbed him by the head when he was pleasing her, but she did it every time. She couldn't help herself; it intensified her orgasm and she didn't plan on stopping. "It's not funny." He narrowed his eyes at her and then answered his ringing phone. "Hudson, my man what's up."

Sutton looked up at him and she could see traces of her all around his mouth as he stood there talking to her dad.

"I know y'all hear us out here ringing the doorbell. Y'all need to stop being nasty, that's why y'all got babies on the way now." Kahleno could hear the smile in Hudson's voice. He was happy to be a grandfather and had announced it on more than one occasion.

"That's your nasty ass daughter." Sutton gasped and threw the pillow that was closest to her at him and he laughed. "Give me a minute to brush my teeth and I'm coming. Wait, you gotta key, just open the door we'll be up in a minute."

"That key is for emergencies but with your permission we're coming in."

Sutton had given her dad a key when she first moved in permanently with Kahleno, with his permission. They decided to rent out her place until they decided what they were going to do about a house because neither of theirs were big enough for their growing family. Kahleno wanted at least a six-bedroom home to accommodate their kids, current and future.

Kahleno went in the bathroom right as he heard the alarm chirp to get himself presentable and handle his hygiene. When he came out of the bathroom Sutton was laying on her stomach lightly snoring. He grabbed her leg and shook her until she was glaring at him.

"Don't fucking look at me like that, didn't the doctor tell you to stop sleeping on your stomach. You starting to piss me off with that shit Sut." Kahleno fussed and Sutton rolled her eyes. She was a stomach sleeper and it was hard to adjust to not sleeping that way.

"Stop yelling at me I'm trying." She scooted out of the bed to go relieve herself and shower real quick. She knew that Kahleno wasn't letting her go to sleep and she hadn't seen her dad in a couple of weeks. Whenever she would call him, he always sounded busy. Especially since he joined the Maler empire, at least the legal side of it.

Kahleno shook his head and made his way into the living room with his father in law. He walked in the room he used for his office and grabbed the ring box that he had just got from the jeweler the other day. He knew that Sutton would be a while, so he wanted to share it with Hudson and formally ask for his permission.

They had talked about them possibly getting married, but he wanted to formally do it the right way. When he walked in the house, he was surprised to see Pebbles there with Hudson and the solemn look on their faces let him know that this visit had the potential to end badly.

"The fuck going on?" Kahleno stopped but Hudson's eyes was on what was in his hands.

"What's that?" he pointed to the bag with a smile on his face.

"You first." Kahleno made his way to where Hudson was, he took a look up the stairs to make sure that Sutton wasn't coming.

"I need to tell Sutton something that she may not like." Kahleno dropped his head and shook it. He didn't want Sutton stressing over nothing even if it had to do with her father.

"She's pregnant and you know how she gets."

"I know that, but I can't keep hiding shit from her Kahleno. After all that shit went down with your family it had me thinking. Life is too short to dwell on the past. I will always love Nova with everything in me, but she's gone and it's time for me to move on. I've been hiding my feelings for this woman for so long and I don't want to hurt her like that anymore."

Kahleno understood where Hudson was coming from, he just didn't see Sutton taking this very well. He sighed heavily as he prepared himself for what was to come. Deciding to let them handle their family issues and just be there if Sutton needed him, he handed the box with the ring in it over to Hudson.

Slowly pulling the ring out he admired the six-carat princess cut diamond ring. The simplicity of the ring was breathtaking and right up Sutton's alley. It was everything that she would have ever wanted, and Hudson was more than pleased that Kahleno was going to be the one to give it to her.

"You did an amazing job son." Hudson stood and pulled Kahleno in for a hug.

Peebles couldn't help but cry as the two men embraced. She knew the struggles that the relationship had at the beginning and she prayed that her and Sutton would have the same outcome. Having been around Sutton her whole life, she knew how she could be, so she was prepared for the worse.

"Thank you, I can't wait to put it on her finger." Kahleno beamed and then looked at Hudson. "With your permission of course."

"I wouldn't have it any other way."

The two men embraced again and then Kahleno jogged back up the stairs to replace the ring back where it was. He rejoined them and said a little prayer that Sutton wouldn't spaz out too much.

The three talked until they heard the room door open and shut. Hudson and Pebbles both swallowed hard and looked at each other. Hudson reached over and grabbed Pebbles hand in his and squeezed a little.

Sutton walked down the stairs one at a time like she was in a runway show. Her beautiful sandy brown hair flowed down her back and bounced with each step she took. The smile on her face showcased the dimples that buried deep in her round face. She was beautiful, there was no denying that and Kahleno couldn't wait to make her his wife.

"Hey daddy." Sutton walked over to hug her father and stopped in her tracks. "Hey Pebbles, what you doing here?" the smile on her face slowly faded as she looked down at the two holding hands. Pebbles quickly drew her hand back making Hudson glare at her.

"Honey we would like to talk to you, you should sit down." He said to Sutton as he snatched Pebbles hand back into his. The way he saw it he deserved to be happy and he prayed that his daughter was happy for him.

"What's going on?" Sutton crossed her arms across her chest and leaned her weight to favor one hip over the other. "Daddy? Pebbles?"

"Sit down sweetheart and we can talk about this like a family." Hudson tried to reason with her, but the way Sutton saw it, they had done enough talking and whatever else they were involved in.

"No I'm good where I am."

"Sutton come here." Kahleno said begging her to calm down while reaching out for her. She rolled her eyes at him because he was too calm for her liking, indicating that he probably knew about whatever the fuck was going on. "Sutton...come...here!" Kahleno said with a little more authority this time and she smacked her lips and stomped over to her like he asked.

"Listen honey," Hudson started as he watched Kahleno whisper something in her ear that relaxed her for a minute. "We don't know how to tell you this..."

"We?" she cut him off. "What do you mean we?"

"Sutton calm the fuck down and listen." Kahleno whispered in her ear making her shoulders shutter. She loved when he talked to her like that and often did little things so that he would. The seat of her fresh thongs were getting ruined by the second.

"Me and Pebbles have been seeing each other for a while now. We love each other and we want to be together. I hated keeping this from you Sutton, but we didn't know how you would react," Hudson started before Pebbles joined in.

"*We* didn't want to hurt you or for you to think that we were betraying Nova, it just kind of happened. At first, we were both ashamed and then it became normal and now, here we are." She searched Sutton's eyes for some kind of understanding, but she got nothing.

"Baby please don't be mad; I will always love your mother..."

"We will always love Nova," Pebbles butted in.

"Yes, but she's gone, and I still have a life to live and..." was all he got out before Sutton took off running up the stairs.

"Oh no," Pebbles covered her face and broke down crying while Hudson comforted her. Kahleno hated that Sutton reacted like she did but he almost expected it. Pebbles was her mother's friend and even though it seemed like it was messed up, Kahleno could see how it happened.

"I'll go talk to her, give me a minute." Kahleno took the stairs two at a time.

When he got to the door, he held his ear to the door expecting to hear crying or sniffling, but he didn't hear neither. When he opened the door, Sutton was sitting in the middle of the bed with the bag of chips that she kept on her nightstand for him midnight cravings.

"He still here?" Sutton asked and Kahleno looked at her like she was crazy. "What?"

"Are you okay?" Kahleno leaned against the door with his hands in his pockets, she was starting to freak him out, she was too calm for his liking. He was waiting for her to scream, throw something or her favorite thing, to cry but she was stone faced.

"Yeah." Was all she offered.

"You want to talk about it?"

"Talk about what? They're together and I'm kind of happy for them. My dad deserves to be happy; I know that he's not going to be alone forever. I get that. I just hate that they felt like they had to lie to me." She shrugged her shoulders. "I know my dad loved my mother, there is no doubt in my mind and Pebbles loved her too."

"So why did you run off?"

"Because he gave me all that hell about being with you and here, he was hiding his relationship from me." She giggled. "I'm making him sweat. I'll talk to him another time." She shrugged her shoulders. "It's his turn to get the cold shoulder."

Kahleno couldn't believe what he was hearing, he couldn't do anything but laugh and shake his head. They were down there freaking out because they thought she was mad and didn't approve of their relationship and she was fine with it just being an asshole.

"If you don't get your pretty petty ass down those stairs and talk to your father." He laughed at the smile that spread across her face. "Pebbles is having a complete break down right now." Kahleno pointed to the door and Sutton felt bad a little.

"She's knows how I am, if I was mad about it, I would have flipped the hell out not run to the room." She shook her head and climbed out of the bed. Kahleno opened the door and Sutton took the stairs to rejoin her father and Pebbles. "Where y'all going?" she asked when she saw them headed to the door.

"Sutton I'm sorry, if you want us to break it off then I will. You know I love you, but I fell in love with your father too, but I don't want to ruin our relationship. I love you that much." Pebbles sobbed and Sutton felt like shit for not taking the severity of the situation in to consideration.

"No the hell you're not, Sutton is my daughter and I love her to death, but life is too short to be anything but happy and I'm happy with you," Hudson said to Pebbles. He wasn't trying to disrespect his daughter, but she was grown and starting her own family and he was trying to build one with Pebbles.

"It was a joke," Sutton said and they both looked at her. "I'm not mad, I just really hate that you felt like you had to hide it from me. I know that you both loved my mother, and you love me. Dad you deserve to be happy and Pebbles so do you." Sutton smiled.

"We never messed around when Nova was alive and—"

"Stop, I know that." Sutton stopped her. "Just don't hide things from me, we're a family. We we're before this." She waved her hand back and forth between the two of them. "We should be honest with each other."

"I love you baby." Hudson pulled her in for a hug.

"I love you too daddy." She hugged her father and then let him go. Pebbles stood off to the side nervously. "Nothing's gonna change Pebbles, I promise we're good."

"I know I will never take your mother's place and I'm not trying to Sutton—" Pebbles started, and Sutton cut her off again.

"Oh shut up Pebbles." Sutton placed her hands on her hips.

"Now you wait a damn minute missy." Pebbles mimicked Suttons' gesture and Sutton laughed.

"There's my Pebbles." She wrapped her hands around her and the two embraced. Hudson stood back and admired the two women that he loved the most.

CHAPTER THIRTEEN

Differences
"Didn't I tell yo ass not to hurt my got damn sister," Vinny said as he stepped aside and let Cassidy in the house. The phone was up to his ear as he glared at Cassidy. "Cami let me call you back, I gotta cuss this nigga out."

"You said that last time Vinny and never hit me back. Keep playing with me and you gone make me show my ass. Real talk nigga!" she yelled through the phone.

The two had just started back talking. After the whole Trouble situation, Vinny called himself cutting her off until she started talking to another man. He shut it down so quick and here they were.

"Shut yo baldheaded ass up. You sound like a nigga." Vinny shook his head. "I said I'm calling you back when I get this nigga out my house."

"Yeah, well I'm on my way over there cause I don't believe you." She hung up the phone and Vinny looked at it making sure that she really hung up on him. Sliding his phone back in his pocket he gave Cassidy his undivided attention.

"Where she at?"

"Don't worry about it, I told you if you wasn't serious then leave her the fuck alone." Vinny pointed at Cassidy.

"That shit threw me for a fucking loop, had me looking at her side ways. What exactly did you want me to do?" Cassidy said calmly. "What kind of woman keeps a kid from a man?"

"The kind that does what's best for her fucking child," Key said walking into the house giving Vinny the side eye.

"Don't fucking look at him like that, shit I was in here minding my business and he showed up. I was taking up for your retarded ass, I won't do that shit no more." Vinny flipped his sister off and started texting away at his phone.

"Since you in my business, I'm telling Camila that the Jayla bitch was over here last night," Key said calling Cami by her real name.

"You do that shit and I'ma fuck you up Key real talk. You on that good ol bullshit. Cassidy please take her back there and give her some dick or something. She's been a royal bitch since y'all been fighting."

Key mushed Vinny in the head as he walked by to go in the room. She didn't really want to talk to Cassidy, but him being in her presence was wearing her down. Dodging him had been her thing lately because she knew the minute that he was in front of her he would wear her down.

"Why are you here?" her harsh tone cut through the silence that surrounded them. She didn't need him judging her for her past and she didn't feel like explaining to him why she made the decisions that she made, and she wasn't going to. She had done that enough.

"I didn't fuck Piper." Was the first thing out of his mouth. He felt the need to clear that up real quick. "She was at the bar when I was there, and we talked about you and Saque. We got drunk and she was scared to go home so I offered her my couch. I slept in my room and she slept on the couch. Nothing more, nothing less."

"You want me to believe that?"

"Whether you believe it or not is not up to me, that's on you but that's my truth and that's all I know."

"Why were y'all talking about me?" she placed her hand on her hips as she looked in to his chocolate face. She hated how handsome he was and how the smell of his cologne always gets her juices flowing.

"Because I didn't understand how you could just keep a man from his child like that." Cassidy answered honestly. "I didn't see you like that, so when I heard it, I reacted. In my mind it made you look sneaky and selfish. My Key is none of those things, so I was shocked. She helped me see the other side of things, by talking her through her problems with Saque."

"I was so scared; you don't know the hell that man put me through. It was like I was a prisoner in my own got damn relationship. When my mother died, we didn't have anything, I mean nothing, and he knew that. He came into my life and helped me and Vinny out. He became like a savior to me." The tears pooled in her eye lids. Cassidy wanted to get up and be there for her, but he felt like she needed him to listen. "So when my savior turned into the devil himself, I didn't know what to do. I had gotten comfortable with the life that I was living, and I was able to do for Vinny. We were finally happy and then the first thing I do that he didn't want me to do he started to dangle it in my face, then when he knew I was dependent on him the controlling stuff came."

Cassidy couldn't take it anymore he grabbed her by the waist and pulled her to him. Sliding her in his lap and wrapping his hands around her waist.

"It was like he thrived off of controlling me, I couldn't take living like that, so I met someone that made me feel free. I ended up cheating on him and he caught us after a while. He shot him and almost beat me to death." Key sniffled. "When I was in the hospital, I found out I was a few weeks pregnant. I knew that I didn't want a man like that to raise my son, I know that was a selfish decision to make but I just couldn't fathom having to co-parent with him."

Cassidy felt sorry for her; he knew the basics of their relationship, but this was the first time that he's seeing how it affected her. It made him feel like a dick.

"What about the shit he said bout you taking your clothes off for men that could possibly be his dad?" The prostitute thing was bothering Cassidy more than he would like to admit but now was the time to ask to clear the air.

"He said that to piss you off." She shook her head. "After I had Kane and him and his sister blackballed me, I was struggling to take care of him, but I refused to ask them for anything. This girl whose hair I braid told me about webcamming. It's like Stripping but it's on the computer screen. I didn't get naked, but I just stripped down to my thongs on camera and men paid to see me."

"Who in the fuck gone pay to see someone strip that they can't touch?" That whole idea was absurd to Cassidy.

"You'd be surprised. I made hella money. I did that but when Vinny found out that's when he went out and started working for y'all. I stopped and started doing hair out of the house and we made it work."

"Why didn't you say that the night of the hair show?" Cassidy felt like a lot could have been resolved if she would have just come out and talked to him.

"Because at the time I didn't want to be near Saque and I didn't want him questioning me about Kane. My son didn't need to hear that or meet his father under those circumstances."

"So now what?" Cassidy asked.

"He rolled up on me and the girls eating, we got into it but by the end we realized that we both hurt each other and while we may never like each other, we needed to come to a common ground for Kane."

Cassidy didn't know if he liked the fact that she had a sit down with this nigga. He could see it in his eyes that he still had some feelings for Key. Kane was his son thought so

Cassidy told himself that he would play the backfield until lines were crossed and then he would step in.

"When you gone let him meet him?"

"After the DNA test comes back. It was gone be before then, but the nigga tried to play me so now it's gone be on my terms." Key smirked before she got serious again. "I'm not perfect Cassidy, I told you that before. My past is my past and I grew from it, I won't apologize for it either and if that's something you can't accept then I get it but let me know now."

"Akiya, I've just always been a man that didn't believe in wasting his time. I've always known what I wanted, and I went after it. When I met you, you met everything that I had ever asked for in a woman." He leaned up and crashed his lips against hers. "I just never took into consideration that what made you who you are may not be as pretty as what I see now. For that I'm sorry."

Tears flew down Key's face, she felt so connected to Cassidy. She couldn't fully say that she loved him yet, but she was damn sure moving in that direction. Everything that he is, is everything that she wanted.

"What now?"

"I wanna try this again. Everything is out in the open and I just want us to build from that. I mean that's if that's okay with you?" Key stared into his eyes and nodded her head. She didn't want anything else in this world. "Aight well let's go, I got to get to Kahleno's. Mama coming home today and if you ain't there when she gets there, I will never hear the fucking end of it." Key giggled.

Siya was everything, she loved the advice she gave them when it came to her sons. Everything she said was right and she would forever be grateful.

"Cool, let me change real quick, Kane is already there. He called Sutton and asked if he could come over with Kahlil and she said yeah."

"So you just doing drop offs now? You wasn't gone stay?"

"No I didn't want to see you, but I'm glad I did." Cassidy slapped her on the ass and watched as she walked to the back to change her clothes. He had half the mind to go in there with her and get him a make-up quickie, but they had a lifetime to do that. She wasn't getting away from him again and he put that on his unborn kids. Key was what he wanted, what he deserved, and he was glad that he found her.

"This damn girl gone drive me crazy," Vinny said casually walking back in the living room.

"Who? Jayla?"

"Fuck naw, if she didn't suck my dick the way she do I wouldn't even fuck with her clingy ass but I'm talking about Cami."

"I meant to ask you what was up with that, I thought y'all were cooling it."

"We was but that's my baby. She thought she was going to be running into the sunset with another nigga and I wasn't having it." The sneaky smirk that appeared on his face made Cassidy laugh. "Shit I swooped in and shut that shit down."

"So you gone settle down with her?"

"Hell nah, a nigga too young for that but I'ma keep my shit out of her face until a nigga ready."

"That's a dangerous game you playing, you gone end up hurting her to the point where she'll be gone for good," Cassidy warned.

"Mind yo muthafuckin business Cassidy and keep that smile on my sister's face. Cause the next time y'all into it and she come around here with her shit I'm gone shoot her mean ass."

"You ain't gone do shit." Cassidy laughed and leaned back on the couch waiting for Key to get done so they could go and welcome his mom home properly. He was happy he got his girl back, he planned on making their shit solid.

CHAPTER FOURTEEN

Family Ties

Kahleno, Cassidy, and AD rushed around the house making sure that everything was set up just the way their mother would like it. After complaining and threatening every person on the staff, Siya had finally got her departure papers.

Mega gave the boys the task of planning a welcome home get together for his wife with just immediate family. They had whipped up some food and had Sutton and Icelynn decorate. The only thing they were waiting on was Siya to make her grand entrance.

Ding dong! The doorbell sounded and Kahleno rushed to the door praying that it wasn't his father. He was supposed to call him before he got here so he could make sure they were ready. When he got to the door, he looked through the peep hole and saw that it was Officer Barrett, one of the officers on his payroll.

Kahleno swung the door open and was almost knocked down by Kahlil running full force and tackling his legs before taking off in the direction of laughing. When he looked back up Karson made herself known. The worried look on her face let Kahleno know that he wasn't gonna like what she was about to say.

"Hey, sorry we're late but Kahlil took all day finishing his breakfast." Karson smiled nervously.

"The fuck going on?" Kahleno was no fool, he already knew that Barrett was the man that Karson had been dealing with. He just wondered when they were gonna tell him. He wasn't mad at all, Karson deserved happiness just like he did but he wanted to know that she wasn't with any shit.

"Kahleno man I didn't even know that she was your son's mother," Barrett said and looked over at Karson who put her head down. "Me and her met at her job, I was called out because someone tried to break in. When I got there something drew me to her and we just clicked. Shit felt good." He smiled and Kahleno could see that he really cared about Karson, that was a good sign. "She didn't bother to tell me who she was associated with." He gritted.

"I didn't think it was important, DeShawn," she said calling him by his first name. "Hell I didn't know you were connected to him. It's not my place to announce who my son's father is to every man I meet." She rolled her eyes.

Kahleno was a very well-known man, which interfered

with most relationships she tried to start, and he knew that. So when she met a cop, she figured that it would be her one chance to be with someone that wasn't connected to her son's father. Imagine her surprise when she introduce him to Kahlil all hell breaks loose.

"So what y'all together?" Kahleno asked.

"Look man, you know we good and we go way back." DeShawn said referring to the fact that he grew up with the Maler Men, they all went to school together. He had gotten in some shit when he was younger and Mega helped him out of it, he left town and went to school to play football while getting his criminal justice degree.

When he blew his knee his senior year, he knew that football wasn't in his future, so he put his degree to use. He went through the academy with Charlotte Mecklenburg Police Department, better known as CMPD and now he was an officer. His plan was to get his shield, but he was a couple years out the academy and needed to work his way up.

After running into Kahleno a while back he was offered a job on their payroll. He owed Mega Maler his life and couldn't turn down the opportunity, so here he was. His love for Karson was strong and he prayed that this wouldn't affect his business relationship with Kahleno.

"Nigga I know that," Kahleno said wishing he would get to the point.

"I didn't know that she was ya babymoms until I saw your son. I ain't on no disrespectful bullshit but I love Karson and

I want to be with her. I just don't want it to interfere with our shit that we got going on."

Karson hated that Kahleno had so much power over everything that surrounded her. From Kahlil, to her feelings and now to the man that she was using to get over him. Although she did have love for DeShawn, if Kahleno asked her to come back to him she would do it in a heartbeat. That was just the god's honest truth.

"It's cool." Kahleno shrugged and both DeShawn and Karson looked shocked. "Listen, what me and Sutton got going is amazing, never felt anything like it in this world. I love that woman more than anything outside of my son and my babies she got growing in her stomach."

"Babies?"

"Yeah, we got twins on the way and I plan to make her my wife before she gives birth." Kahleno smiled and DeShawn gave him dap.

"Wow congratulations." Even though she still loved Kahleno, she was genuinely happy for him. She secretly still wished that it was her that he spoke of like that, but she came to grips with the fact that she ruined that. When her eyes met DeShawn's her heart fluttered, not like when she was with Kahleno, but her heart definitely flutters. She was happy.

"Thanks and congrats to the two of you as well." Kahleno nodded. "I'm good. As long as you treat my son like's he's yours and don't put your hands on him we good."

"How you gone say for him to treat him like his own but

say he can't discipline him in the same sentence? Kahlil is bad as hell."

"Easy." Kahleno shrugged. "Kahli is my problem and D is a man before anything else, so he knows where I'm coming from."

"Oh yeah because I would be the same way if someone touched my little man." He rubbed Karson's little belly and Kahleno smiled.

Wondering if DeShawn knew that Karson was trying to say that his baby was Kahleno's all this time. Or if he knew that she tried to fuck him that night? He could seriously burst her bubble, but he decided against it. He wanted her to be happy even If he didn't truly believe the façade.

"That's what's up. I'm praying for a boy and a girl. Then I'm knocking her ass up right after and if it's another girl we'll stop." Kahleno showed all thirty-two teeth.

"Kahleno I heard you talking that bullshit." Sutton said coming around the corner. She already told him that she wasn't having a bunch of kids, but he had it in his mind that he was. "Oh hey Karson and..."

"DeShawn Barret." He nodded. "Nice to finally put a name with a face. This man talks so highly of you."

"I've trained him to keep all the bad things to himself." Sutton smiled and DeShawn and Karson laughed. Kahleno popped her on the ass and she leaned up and kissed him and walked away.

"We'll we're gonna get going. I know Kahlil ain't trying to

come home no time soon so just call me before you bringing him home and tell Siya I said I'm glad she's feeling better."

"Aight I will." Kahleno and DeShawn said a few more words to each other before they parted ways and Kahleno went back to what he was doing.

~

"Mega what are you up to?" Siya asked as they drove down the highway. He had been looking at his phone the entire time since they left the hospital. She had a whole conversation by herself because he was too busy checking his phone.

"Nothing woman, just sit back and enjoy the sunshine." Mega smiled. They were almost home, and the boys just texted that everything was done, and they were waiting. "I'm glad you're coming home."

"I can't tell, I've been asking you forever to bring me home. I almost broke out and came to see if you were living life without me and that's why you didn't want me home," she joked.

"You are my life, my everything. Why when I can't live without you?" Mega grabbed her thigh and gave it a squeeze.

Things for the Maler family had been hectic to say the least. Mega was a firm believer in everything happens for a reason and he felt like everything that happened to their family made them stronger than ever.

"I love you Mega Maler."

"I love you too and I'm sorry you had to go through all of this. Just know that I will spend the rest of my life making it up to you."

Siya knew that his words were true, she hated what her family had been through, but she didn't blame Mega. There was only one woman to blame and her name was Ziva Whyte, she couldn't wait to get her hands on her. She hated everything about that woman.

"Where we going baby?"

"Stopping by Kahleno's house." Mega glanced from the road for a second and then turned into Kahleno's long drive way.

"I hope my babies are in here." Siya reached for her seatbelt and pulled it off. She still had the cast on her leg, but she could get around with it. The doctor had just released her to put weight on it and she had been hobbling along ever since.

The minute they got to the door Siya put her ear up to it and noticed that it was kind of quiet and instantly got upset thinking that Kahlil wasn't here. When she turned the door knob she realized that it was open.

"SURPRISE!" everyone yelled the minute her face came into view. Tears rushed to her eyes and down her face as she looked at her son's and the lovely women that they had started to build with. Siya knew that she was blessed, despite everything that she had been through, the woman was blessed.

"I should kick y'all asses." She cried as she walked the rest of the way into the house. Making her rounds hugging everyone, Mega stood back, and watched while Siya cried tears of joy. She missed her family, even though she saw them when they came to visit it was different. "Where's my babies?" she fussed.

She had grown to love Isis and Kane like they were her own and she called them as such. They were the first one's that she wanted to see after been cooped up in the hospital for weeks.

"They're in that game room." Sutton pointed down the hall to the game room that Kahleno had built for Kahlil when he first bought the house. Siya nodded her head and headed to the back where the kids where.

The rest of the day they all sat around and enjoyed each other. They talked and laughed, Siya got to know more about the women who had bullied their way into her boy's hearts. She was happy to see her family happy.

CHAPTER FIFTEEN

*C*ommunication

"I don't think I want to do this Cas." Key whined from the sidelines with Cassidy.

She knew that when he suggested that they go and talk to Saque that she wouldn't want to go through with it. Even though she had decided to let him be a part of Kane's life, she still hated him. It was something about the thought of him being in her life again that rubbed her the wrong way.

"Do you trust me?" Cassidy's answer was simple, but Key knew better than the think that was all it meant.

They had really been getting to know each other and she loved every moment of it. He had a smart mouth but that was one of the things that Key liked about Cassidy. He didn't bite his tongue and he kept her laughing.

"Yeah but what does that have to do with me not wanting to sit down with Saque and Piper?" Key snarled her nose up.

Even though Cassidy explained to her that nothing happened with him and Piper she still felt a way about it. Piper gave her a sneaky vibe and from what she had heard from Sutton and Icelynn she wasn't a really good person. She didn't trust her and felt like she shouldn't have been in that close of a proximity of her man.

"Don't start, I already talked to you about that." Cassidy smirked and shook his head. Piper was Piper and yes, he had a soft spot for her, and he couldn't explain it but that's as far as it went. His attention was on Key and Key alone. "You scared she gone get some of your sweet meat?" Cassidy covered his mouth with his fist and laughed.

"Yeah and I'll shoot you both, and you know I will."

"You ain't gone do shit. But real shit, ain't no one worried about that girl." Cassidy shrugged his shoulders and then focused back on the field. Kane's championship game was today, and he thought that it would be a good idea if Key invited Saque to come see him play. "And this is a good thing. It shows that you're trying so if he fucks up at least you did your part. This man deserves to build a relationship with his kid until he proves he doesn't."

"Listen to you sounding all philosophical and shit." Key leaned up to kiss him, but he lightly mushed her head away and she giggled. "Stop bae, give me a kiss." Key laughed and then connected her lips with Cassidy's.

"Seriously, just give the man a chance. I know y'all been

through some shit but y'all created a life together and I think it's worth it to at least give the man a chance to do right."

"But what if he doesn't?" Key was skeptical of the whole wanting to get to know his son. She was sure that Saque had an ulterior motive, she just wanted to see it show.

"Then I'll beat his ass," Cassidy said simply.

Cassidy looked on as he watched Kane do a spin move out of a tackle and run until the coach blew the whistle. They were doing warm-ups and he always made it his business to stand on the sidelines and Kane had grown accustomed to seeing him there. When he walked back, Kane smirked and threw his head up and Cassidy followed suit.

Cassidy had grown to love Kane. He was a handful and he had a hand problem with a heap of anger to match, but Cassidy was working hard to steer him in a better direction. The fact that they both love the game of football solidified their bond even more.

"He listens to you." Key interrupted the thoughts that were flowing through her own head. "You taught him that last night." The smile that spread on her face brought one to Cassidy's as he watched Kane do the move that he showed him.

"Kanaan is mature for his age, and I talk to him as such." Cassidy slipped his hands in his pockets and continued to watch.

When they were done warming up, the coach told them to go and get water. Kane ran right in the direction of Cassidy and his mother. Kane was fond of the man that his mother had chosen to spend time with, and he was happy he was in their lives.

He had never seen his mother this happy before and he appreciated the man for making that happen. Kane also liked that fact that he made time for him. If they weren't playing the game or working on school work, Cassidy had him in the backyard running drills and Kane loved it. Cassidy respected him and that respect was returned ten times fold.

"Yo I broke dudes ankles." Kane said as he smiled up at Cassidy waiting for his approval.

"I saw that shit but you still bouncing off of your heel, remember what we worked on last night. If you push off of the balls of your feet you get more momentum." Kane look down and planted the top of his foot into the ground and then pushed off of it like he was about to run. It felt good so he smirked at Cassidy and nodded his head. "I'll never steer you wrong my dude." They dapped each other up.

"What the hell he doing here?" Kane snarled his nose up at the man that his mother explained to him was his father. He wasn't too fond of him because it seemed that every time, he came around it darkened his mother's mood and he hated that. When his mother hurt, he hurt.

"Kanaan Delaney!" Key scolded. Cassidy chuckled making Key flash a hateful glance his way. "Watch your mouth, he wanted to come and support you. He's trying to get to know you."

"I don't want to know him, I got Cassidy." Kane looked up

at Cassidy right as Saque walked up with Piper who had a smile on her face.

She and Saque had just made love before they left the house which was why they were late. They had been getting along great since everything unfolded. The only thing she couldn't get was Sutton to forgive her, she was only privy to information about her through her social media and she hated that. She wanted to be there for her through her pregnancy, but Sutton wasn't having it. She claimed that she couldn't entertain anything that could possibly disrupt her peace while she was carrying her babies.

Although Piper wanted to object and force Sutton to talk to her, she knew that she didn't deserve it. After everything unfolded, she had time to think and she realized that she really was a shitty friend and she hated herself for it but all she could do was apologize and move forward, with hopes that Sutton would do the same. She really missed her friend.

"Hey y'all," Piper spoke softly making Key scoff. She hated that Piper played the innocent roll when she knew that she was anything but. The vibes that she got from her threw her off every time and she could only tolerate her in small segments.

"Hey," Cassidy said with a head nod.

"What's up my man?" Saque held his hand out and Kane looked at it with a mug on his little handsome face.

Kane looked up at Cassidy who was trying not to laugh. Saque notice the gesture and it burned him up that his son didn't know who he was and turned to another man for guidance, a man whose blood didn't flow through him.

"Come on man, what we talk about?" Cassidy looked down at Kane and a smirk appeared on his face. When he asked Cassidy if he had to meet his father, Cassidy told him to give the man a chance and if he didn't do right that the two would jump him.

"Can we just skip to the second part?" Key wore a confused look on her face because she had no idea what the two were talking about, but she knew that it wasn't good by the amused look on both of their faces.

"Yeah ummmm, Kane it's time to get ready. The game is about to start. I'll be in the stands." Key pointed to where they normally sat.

"Okay mom." Kane grabbed her legs and squeezed. He truly loved his mother and all she did for him and even though he showed his ass more times than not, he still wanted her to know that he appreciated her. "Cassidy, I need help?" Kane asked.

"No the hell you don't Kane." Cassidy shook his head and turned to kiss Key. She looked between the two of them and sighed heavily. "I'll meet you up there, you gone be good?" He asked with raised brows.

"Yeah I'm good." Key kissed his lips again and Cassidy didn't miss the sour look on Saque's face so for good measure Cassidy leaned down and stuck his tongue in Key's mouth and she accepted.

"Ewwwww!" Kane laughed breaking up the pair. Cassidy

chuckled and followed Kane to the field to help with his pads. Key watched as the two walked off, she loved their relationship but the two of them together were trouble and she knew that she had her hands full.

When she turned around to walk off, she was met with Saque's menacing stare. It was mixed with anger, agitation, annoyance, and envy sat high on the list of things that radiated from his eyes. He never thought that he would be anywhere near the woman who caused him so much pain, let alone be here with her, his son, and her new man.

Saque knew that he didn't have a leg to stand on so he couldn't react how he wanted to, so he tried his best to calm down.

"Why are you looking at me like that?" Key asked as Piper noticed her man's change in demeanor.

"Is that what you do in the presence of my son?" he asked incredulously.

"Saque no one wants to hear that." Key waved her hand in the air dismissively. "We're here to watch Kane play football, not worry about what I do with my nigga. If you can't handle it then maybe you should leave."

Key was waiting for his shit to show; he had been playing *Mr. Cool* for too long and she knew that it was only a matter of time before the real him reared his ugly head. He glared at her and she wasn't in the mood to deal with his shit, so she headed towards the bleachers with him following close behind.

His eyes horned in on the way her ass giggled in the tight

black jeans that she wore. He couldn't help but flash back to the times where he used to watch as his dick slid in and out of her while she arched her back just the way he liked it. He missed their action in the bedroom and the mere thought of her being with anyone else infuriated him. He hated her and loved her at the same time.

Piper cleared her throat when he stopped mid stride, she followed his eyes and they were glued to Key's ass. Saque looked back and offered up a soft smile but he didn't get anything in return.

"Chill baby, I'm just pissed that my son don't even know me. I should be out there helping him get ready for his game. Not some random ass nigga," Saque fussed turning his attention to the field.

"Yeah and you got all of that from the crack of her ass." Piper tilted her head. She knew there was history there, but they were supposed to be building a future, so respect was a must whether his baby moms was there or not.

"It wasn't like that baby, come on." He reached out and grabbed Piper's hand and the two walked up to the stairs and sat behind Key.

Saque watched on as envy burned its way through his heart. Cassidy was out there showing Kane something on the football field. The coach even came over and started talking to Cassidy like he was his father.

"He does know that's not his son, right?" Saque leaned down and said to Key who rolled her eyes and sighed.

"Yes, he's well aware. He's the only reason I've been in

contact with you so some gratitude would be nice." Key rolled her eyes.

"Gratitude! Gratitude! You have got to be shitting me!" Saque scoffed. "You are the reason that I'm not down there with him. It's because of you I was in jail and missed out on five years of my son's life. It's your fault he doesn't know who his father is," Saque said louder than he intended drawing a small audience.

Key pulled her bottom lip into her mouth and nibbled on it. She was trying hard not to give him what he wanted, but she was so close to showing her ass. As if on que, Cassidy began to make his way to where Key was.

"I didn't put that gun in your hand, I didn't make you take that shot. I didn't force you to be a controlling asshole who threw hissy fits when you didn't get your way. I'm sorry I wasn't built to be submissive, it's not in me. I should have left you long before I cheated, and I know that, and for that I'm sorry, but I won't take responsibility for the rest of your baggage." Key turned enough so that she was facing him, and his eyes went to her breast.

This time Cassidy saw him and stepped into view. "Eye problem nigga? Those belong to me. The only thing that you have with Key is Kane, so long as you know that shit can go smooth. Shit happened and you both were wrong, now you can get over it or we can end this shit now." Cassidy's tone was low so that only they could hear, but it held enough power to get his point across.

"This ain't got anything to do with you." Saque tried his

best to sound confident, but it definitely didn't come across as such.

"It has everything to do with me because while you walking around bitching about not knowing your son, I'm getting to know him and he's a damn good kid. Maybe if you take some of the energy you using to point fingers and worrying about Key and direct it towards your son you would get somewhere with him." Cassidy pointed to the field. "He ain't a dumb kid and he loves his mother. You doing this bull-shit ain't gone win you over with him. He can sense his moth-er's vibe change when you're around and that makes him look at you like the enemy instead of like a part of him. You can keep on with the bullshit if you want to and lose out, but I can go ahead and let you know my patience is wearing really thin." Cassidy turned around signaling that the conversation was over.

The smile that slowly spread on Key's face couldn't be missed. Everything heated up in her while Cassidy handled that situation and she couldn't wait to show him how much she appreciated him stepping in like that. Cassidy was in a league of his own and she was happy that he was on her arm.

"Keep biting down on your lip like that and you gone start some shit." Cassidy leaned over and said causing her to giggle. She really was starting to fall for this man, she just prayed he felt what his actions showed.

"You okay?" Piper leaned over and asked him. He was tense and with every word that Cassidy spoke he squeezed her hand a little more.

"Yeah I'm good." He leaned over and kissed her lips relaxing some. What Cassidy said was right, he needed to put more energy into getting to know his son instead of worrying about him and Key. That was easier said than done, but he would try. Plus, Piper was a good girl and she loved him. Key wasn't worth losing that, not for someone who cheated on him. *Right?*

"Go! Go! Cut back!" Cassidy cupped his hands around his mouth and yelled. "Yeah boy! Go! Just like that." He jumped up and yelled until Kane hit the end zone. Cassidy threw his hands up and Kane turned around and pointed at him and pumped his fist in the air. Kane was his dude and he was proud to be a part of his life.

CHAPTER SIXTEEN

*M*aler

"Mawmaw when is Isis getting here?" Kahlil asked while he and Kane sat at the table playing the game operation. "Ah hah nigga you lost!"

"Ah hah nigga you ugly!" Kane countered and rolled his eyes. He had just come back from spending the day with his dad and Piper. He didn't want to, but Cassidy thought it was a good idea, so he went with it.

Saque was trying to do better with co-parenting, but Kane could still feel the tension whenever he came around. He would do whatever made his mom happy, so he was giving it a try. Cassidy still promised to help him jump him if he didn't follow through like he said.

"Y'all can't get along for nothing." Siya shook her head.

She got her cast off of her foot the prior week and she

wanted to keep all of her grandkids. Isis and Kane weren't biological, but that didn't mean anything to her. They respected her as their grandmother, and she treated them as such. You would never be able to tell that Isis or Kane didn't have Maler blood.

"He started it!" they said simultaneously causing Siya to laugh.

"Soon as Isis gets here, and Pawpaw gets back, we'll start the cookies and popcorn." They were having a Netflix night with cookies, popcorn, and pizza. She lived for moments like this because there was a time where she didn't think that she would have it.

Just thinking about what she went through with Ziva made her skin crawl. She wanted to get her hands on Ziva in the worse way and she couldn't wait til she got the chance. They had been looking for her everywhere and no one seemed to have a location on her. Not even Marlin, the last he heard she was back in Jamaica.

"And the pizza, I'm hungry," Kane wined and rubbed his stomach.

"You didn't eat over your dad's?"

"No, I don't trust Piper," he said confidently causing Siya to snicker.

"Why not Kanaan?"

"Because she's too nice, she tries way to hard." Kane shook his head and Siya laughed harder.

"She just wants to build a relationship with you. If you and she don't have a relationship it will be hard for her or your daddy to have a relationship. Do you understand?" Siya asked.

She never baby talked to her kids. She gave it to them straight up and she would always ask if they understood, and she didn't plan on being any different with her grands. Kane looked her in the eyes, as he thought about what she said.

"Yeah I get it. If I don't like her then he won't like her." He nodded his head.

"That's exactly right." Nodding, Siya smiled, amazed at how smart all three of them were. Sometimes she was shocked at what came out of their mouths. Not so much Kahlil, she was used to that, but definitely Isis and Kane. She couldn't wait to meet the twins; her family was growing, and she was excited about it.

"Well what if I don't like him?" Kane asked with the most serious face, not a hint of humor insight.

Ding Dong

"Saved by the bell," Siya chuckled and left a confused Kane where he stood as she ran up the stairs to her room to get her purse for the Pizza guy. "Don't y'all open the door!" she yelled out as she grabbed her purse. She meant to have it down there earlier, but she got to talking with the boys and that always threw her off track. "Did y'all hear me?"

When she didn't get an answer, she snatched her purse and took off down the stairs. With everything that the family had been through, she wasn't about to take the chance of someone being down there that could possibly harm them.

Plus, the world wasn't as safe as it used to be when she was a girl.

"Kane? Kahlil?" she yelled as she made her way down the stairs.

"Mawmaw?" she could hear the urgency in his tone and that frightened her. When she got to the bottom of the stairs, she dropped her purse that was in her hand and moved quickly to the door but the gun in her face stopped her.

"Well if it isn't Mrs. Maler, in the flesh." Ziva laughed as she held Kane and Kahlil in one arm and held a gun to their heads with her free hand. "You should teach these little bastards to stay away from the door. It could be danger on the other side." Again she laughed.

"You crazy bitch," Kahlil said as he wiggled to get out of her hold.

"Keep talking you chucky doll," Ziva gritted as she pressed the gun into Kahlil's forehead. He didn't even seem phased by what was going on, him or Kane, but Siya was freaking out. If it was just her, she wouldn't care but these where her grand-kids, her babies.

"How about you let them go and then you'll have me," Siya said looking at Kahlil and Kane who both wore scowls. They kept looking at each other and then at Siya. She hoped that they just remained still and let her handle it, but she had a feeling that wasn't going to happen.

"Or how about I blow their little heads off and make you watch?" Ziva was so tired of Siya always winning. She got the man, the house, the family, and she even got to keep her life after Ziva thought she snatched it away.

"When Mega gets his hands on you..."

"Then what?" Ziva threw her hand in the air and Kahlil and Kane both bit down on her arm so hard that they drew blood. Ziva screamed and went to move her arm but they had a grip on her. She was about to bring the gun down but Siya grabbed her arm and the two started to struggle with the gun.

"Run upstairs boys!" Siya yelled out as she struggled against Ziva, she was taller than Siya, and she was having a hard time getting the gun from her. "GO!" she yelled but they didn't listen.

Kahlil ran to the hall closet where he kept his baseball bat and glove. He grabbed his slugger and swung, barely missing Siya but connecting with Ziva.

"Owww you little bastard!" That gave Siya the upper hand that she needed to get the gun out of her hand. The gun slid across the floor and Siya began to beat the shit out of Ziva, but she wasn't alone.

"You stupid bitch!" Kahlil screamed as he continuously swung his bat against Ziva's legs. Kane went to the kitchen and got the rolling pin that they were gonna use to do the cookies with and began his assault as well. They were all three beating the hell out of her.

"What the fuck?" Mega yelled as he walked through the door and threw the bags that he had down in his hands. He grabbed Ziva by her hair and lifted her off the ground. Siya slipped off, grabbed the boys, and backed away. "You've been a hard muthafucka to find!" Mega growled.

Siya scrambled over and picked up the gun that Ziva had and checked to see if it was loaded even though she knew that it was.

"Boys go upstairs, NOW!" she said, and they looked at her and headed up the stairs, but not before swinging their weapons at Ziva one more time. "Kahlil and Kanaan Maler!" They both smiled and took off up the stairs. Kane loved when she referred to him as a Maler because he felt like one. "It's a shame you're about to die with all that hate in your heart." Siya shook her head.

"I wouldn't be so sure about that." Ziva smiled through bloody lips. Siya had done a number on her once again but she was going to have the last laugh. She would never underestimate a Maler, so she made sure that she wasn't alone.

"Let har guh (Let her go)!" The minute he opened his mouth, he knew exactly who it was. He knew the minute he laid eyes on him that he was a snake and Marlin knew it too, so when he went missing, they knew exactly why.

"Or what bitch?" AD came around the corner and hit Messa over the head with his gun causing him to fall to the ground. "Bitch ass nigga," AD hissed. He watched the unknown man walk up the sidewalk with his gun drawn and when he saw that he was heading to the place where his parents rested their head, he knew he needed to act and quick. "What's up mommy dearest?" He smirked at Ziva who spit at his feet.

AD backed handed the hell out of her, blood flew out of her mouth and she moaned out in pain. "That's no way to treat your one and only son," he laughed again.

"Call your brothers and clean up. Where's Icelynn?"

"She's in the car," AD said as he pulled out his phone and made a few calls. Mega still had Ziva by her hair in the air. She felt like she was being scalped but she wouldn't give them the satisfaction of begging for her life. She got caught slipping, so it is what it is.

Once the kids were gone, Siya walked into the kitchen and grabbed a steak knife, and the minute Ziva was in her sight she plunged the knife into her stomach. Ziva bent over in pain and Siya pulled the knife out and did it again.

"You fucked with my family." She pulled the knife out and plunged it back in even deeper. Ziva cried out. Messa was starting to wake up but AD was standing right there waiting for him with a shot to the head. "I hope you burn in hell bitch." Siya grabbed her throat and stabbed her repeatedly in her neck until she heard a gurgling noise and then nothing at all. She was covered in Ziva's blood.

"Damn Ma, didn't know you had it in you." AD smiled as his mother dropped the knife. "Wait til I tell Cassidy."

As horrible as the scene was, she had never felt so liberated and free. Her family could live in peace, they could go back to living their lives and she was happy about that. She turned and headed up the stairs. When she got in the bathroom she stripped out of her clothes and stepped into the shower.

Allowing the hot stream of water to pour down on her, she let the tears fall that were threatening to. She was releasing all the worry, the fear and the unknown out of her mind and heart.

"That shit was sexy as hell," Mega said entering the bathroom.

"Well you know you bring out the hood in me."

EPILOGUE

"Success!" Kahleno said as he toasted with his brothers by the bar. Tonight was the grand opening of their restaurant and they couldn't be more happy.

They had been through so much crazy, that something good coming into their lives was warranted. Business was booming again; Vinny had moved up and he was working alongside Spiff and they were taking the state of North Carolina by storm. Proud was an understatement.

"This shit is fiyah," Cassidy said looking around.

"Yeah thanks to AD and Icelynn." Kahleno held up his glass of henny.

"Thank you bruh." AD smiled at his accomplishments. He didn't really think that he would be able to pull it off and truth be told they didn't either, but here they were. "Feels good to be a fucking Maler." AD smiled.

"Tell me bout it." Kahleno licked his lips as Sutton twirled around on the floor with her round belly on full display. Words couldn't describe how he felt for that woman and he wasn't gonna try.

"I think I love her," Cassidy said out of the blue and his other two brothers looked at him. Cassidy was always picky when it came to the women in his life. He wasn't one to sleep around and he took his time getting to know the women he dealt with.

Key had come in and showed him things that he didn't know about himself and it opened his eyes to the possibility of what could be with her. He was scared because he had never felt that way about a woman, but Key was perfect for him and he knew that he would be a fool to let her get away.

"Did you tell her that?" Kahleno asked with his eyebrow up.

"Nah not yet, but I will." He smiled as he watched her dance with Kane in the middle of the floor with the rest of the girls. "Matter of fact, let me go do that right now." He walked off from his brothers and headed in the direction of Key.

When she saw him her smile slowly spread across her face and she reached out for him. When he was close, Kane put his hand out and stood in between the two.

"What you want with my mama?" Kane asked.

"I want to love her," Cassidy said with his eyes on Key. Her eyes began to tear up, she knew that she loved Cassidy a long time ago. Granted they were still getting to know each other, but she already loved him. "I love your mom, is that okay my man?"

Kane looked back at his mom and then at Cassidy. He doesn't remember a time when his mom had ever been this happy and he liked Cassidy. He treated him with respect and he actually made time for him. In Kane's eyes that meant more than anything.

"Yeah I'm good with that." The two dapped each other up and he walked over and joined the other kids.

"I guess you heard that Akiya Delaney. Your son said that he was good with me loving you." Cassidy pulled her in his arms and placed a kiss on her lips. "Are you okay with that?" he asked her.

Key looked into the eyes of the man that had come into her life when she least expected it and turned it upside down, in a good way. He made her feel again, trust again. The way he cared for her and her son made it easy for her to return that love to him.

He even went with her to meet up with Saque. Piper was there and they all had a good conversation. They talked about what was good for Kane. Key introduced him to his father, and they had been taking small steps for them to get to know each other. She didn't think any of that would have ever happened if it hadn't been for Cassidy. She was thankful.

"Only if you are okay with me loving you back."

"Sounds damn good to me." His lips pressed against hers as the two slowly moved to the rhythm of the beat while their tongues got reacquainted with each other. They knew that things weren't going to be perfect and that was okay. So long as they got through them together everything would be okay.

"Look at this nigga," AD clowned. He was happy for his brother; he was happy for all of them. They all had been through it and they were moving up.

"Soft ass nigga," Kahleno joked.

"Nigga, I know you ain't talking." AD nudged his brother.

"Well I'm about to make this shit worse." He winked at AD and AD nodded. Kahleno had been waiting all night to figure out when the right time to do this was and now was as good a time as any. When he walked on the dance floor, he wrapped his arms around Sutton and placed his hands on her belly. "You know I love you, right?"

"More than anything in this world and I love you the same." She turned around so that she was facing him. He stared into her eyes; she searched his for what he was thinking, but the second he got down on one knee she knew exactly what was on his mind.

Everyone stopped what they were doing and gave their attention to the couple in the middle of the room. Tears were flying down Sutton's face as she looked into Kahleno's. This was everything that she ever wanted.

"I love you more than anything and I'm so glad that you came into my life. God blessed me the day you walked into that barn. You are an amazing mother figure to my son, and I know that you'll be an even more amazing mother to our kids. I can't wait to meet Nova and Noah, and our lives will be complete. At least until I try and fill you up again," he smirked.

"Watch your got damn mouth Kahleno!" Hudson laughed. Him and Pebbles were great, once they got Sutton's approval they moved in together and Hudson felt whole again. He still missed Nova every day, and to hear that Sutton was naming her daughter after her mother warmed his heart. Everything was good in the world.

"Sorry, Pops," Kahleno chuckled. "I want you to be my wife, no I need you to be my wife." He looked at her. "Will you marry me Sutton Chambers?"

"You didn't even have to ask." She threw her arms around his neck and they shared a passionate kiss. "Yes baby, yes!" she answered, and room erupted in cheers. They danced and celebrated all night. With everything they had been through they deserved it.

~

"*Y*ou ready for this son?" Mega asked as he fixed the knot on his son's tie.

He couldn't have been more proud standing as the best man to his son. When he called him and told him that they just wanted to come to the beach and get married he was all for it. They didn't want all the glitz and glam, they just wanted to say, "I do" and live happily ever after.

"More ready than I ever been about anything. That girl is my life." He smiled.

"Then I know you're ready."

Siya walked into the house and Mega's eyes went straight to her. The way the ocean blue dress hugged her body had his mouth salivating. The curve of her hips and the way her breast sat up nice and perky despite her age had him wanting to take her in one of the rooms of the house and give her a little bit of what he had to offer.

"Damn Pop, you just gone stare ma down like that?" his son laughed.

"Hell yeah, that right there belong to me." He made his way to his wife, engulfed her in his arms, and began to place soft subtle kisses on her neck and shoulders which were exposed due to the dress being off the shoulders. "You... are... so... damn...beautiful," he said between kisses.

"Well thank you my love, but I need you to stop that before you start something that we won't be able to finish."

"Um, I'm standing here; can we not talk like that?" Mega laughed at his son and kissed his wife one more time on her lips.

"Later daddy."

"MA!"

"Okay, okay. I just came in here to tell you that she's here, and she's ready." Siya pulled her son into a hug. She could see and feel the love and admiration that he had for his wife to be. They were happy and so was she. She was biting down on her bottom lip to keep from crying, something she had been doing all day. She placed a kiss on her son's cheek. "I'm so damn proud of you." She choked back the tears. She had been getting her makeup retouched all morning and she was tired of it. "You are going to make an amazing husband and she's one lucky woman."

"I'm the lucky one," he beamed at the thought of the woman that he was about to vow his love to in front of God and his family. "I love you Ma," he said kissing his mother on the cheek.

Looking at her son one more time, Siya slipped out the door making her way to her seat. They didn't want a big wedding, just them.

"Ready?" Mega asked one more time.

"Fuck yeah," his son said as the two men walked outside and down to the flowered arch. When they got to the front, he looked out into the crowd and nodded his head at his brothers. They wasn't mad at all that their brother wanted to keep it simple, they were just happy that he was here.

I found love in you

And I've learned to love me too

Never have I felt that I could be all that you see

It's like our hearts have intertwined and to the perfect harmony

The melodic tunes of Major's song *Why I Love You*, blared through the speakers of AD's beach house. His eyes glossed over when he looked into the eyes of his forever. As her and Isis made their way down the aisle dressed in all white making their light skin look as if it was glowing.

"Wow!" he said under his breath but Mega heard him. He patted his son on the back and AD smiled as he allowed one tear to roll down his face.

This is why I love you

Ooh this is why I love you

Because you love me

You love me

Icelynn's face was full of tears as he slowly made her way down the aisle. Adoreé was her everything, everything that was meant for her in this life was in him and she couldn't be prouder to call herself his wife.

I found love in you

And no other love will do

Every moment that you smile chases all of the pain away

Forever and a while in my heart is where you'll stay

Icelynn looked over to her mother who was sitting on the front row with Siya. She winked at her. She had packed up and relocated for her job. Knowing that her daughter and grand-daughter were in good hands made her feel better about everything. She smiled at Icelynn and then turned her attention to AD who she smiled at.

She had a few conversations with the man that stole her daughter's heart. The respect that she had for him was magnified when she heard Isis call him daddy for the first time. She thanked God on numerous occasions for placing her daughter in the arms of a Maler. To be loved and protected until death would they part.

"This is why I love you," Icelynn sang as she made her way to AD. Looking down at her daughter she smiled when Isis' eyes met hers. "I love you little woman."

"I love you to ma and I love daddy too." She smiled bright

and turned to AD whose face was drenched with tears. He never thought that he would ever have a heart this full. Just knowing that made everything that he had been through in his life worth it, and it showed in this moment.

"Who gives this woman to this man?" the preacher asked and Icelynn's mother stood up.

"I do," she had waited her whole life to say that and she couldn't be prouder to say it on that day.

The pastor prayed and read scriptures, he told them what it would take to be married and made sure that they understood that the covenant they were about to enter into was of God and sacred. When they expressed that they understood he moved on.

"I was told that the couple has written their own vows. If I could get the two of you to hold hands and face each other." They did as they were asked. "Icelynn."

"Everything you are I am; I chose to walk down the aisle to that song because it is who we are. I love you because of how you love me. I can't even put into words the way I feel when I'm in your presence. It's something out of this world. I vow to be your thoughts when you can't think, your heart when you can't feel. I vow to be your peace, your best friend. Whatever you need I promise to be that and so much more."

"Ah shit now, Key you hear that shit. Take notes," Cassidy said from the audience.

"Shut up Cas," she chastised him.

"There is not a minute that goes by that I don't thank God for placing you in our lives, and I'll spend the rest of my life making sure you will never regret having me in yours." Icelynn nodded, letting them know that she was done and then released all the tears that she tried to hold back.

"Adoreé," the pastor gave him the floor. His mother looked at him when he didn't say anything. AD had never been a man of many words but since he had been with Icelynn his communication had increased.

AD looked at Icelynn and then shut his eyes to try and stop the tears that were trying to fall. He was an emotional wreck, but he needed to get this out.

"Before I start, there's something that I need to say to my princess." He let go of Icelynn's hands and kneeled down in front of Isis. "You know you my baby girl, right?" she nodded her head and he smiled. "I can't thank you enough for allowing me to be your daddy. You make my life whole. I don't care if I didn't create you, because our bond was created in here," he tapped his heart, "and," he went into his pocket and pulled out a ring box and opened it up. "I just want to know if you will allow me to be your daddy forever and always?"

Tears traveled down her face as she shook her head up and down, wrapping her arms around his neck and hugging for dear life. AD meant everything to her, he was her hero.

"I love you daddy," she said with her arms around his neck.

"I love you too baby girl." He kissed her cheeks and then faced his forever. There wasn't a dry eye on the beach, including Cassidy, who was trying his hardest not to cry. "Baby, I love you with everything in me. You're right, there are no words to express the love that we share. You came in and loved me when I didn't even love myself." He touched his heart for emphasis and Icelynn lost it. "Everything I am today is because of you. You have already giving me more than I could ever ask for and that's your heart. Even in my darkest hour your smile brought me out of that, and I can never ever repay you for what you've been for me, but I swear on my life I'll spend the rest of my life trying."

Sobs could be heard over the soft music that was playing, the pastor continued on with the service and everyone just looked on in awe of the love that was shown. No one will ever know what the two of them endured together, but they will.

"By the power invested in me I now pronounce to you, Mr. and Mrs. Adoreé Maler. You may now kiss your bride," the Pastor announced, and they embraced for the first time as husband and wife.

"Congratulations Mr. Maler," Icelynn whispered in his ear while he held her in his arms. "You're gonna be a daddy." She smiled as his eyes stretched and he swung her around in the air. Life had a way of challenging you and taking you through things, but it's how you get through those things that makes you who you are.

The Maler family celebrated love, life, and loyalty for the rest of their stay. Things were looking up for them, and they welcomed it.

"Welcome to the family sis." Kahleno and Cassidy walked up and hugged her.

"Don't be trying to boss up on that nigga now," Cassidy said pointing at her and then dapping his brother up.

"Well you know he brings out the hood in me," she winked.

The End

*T*hank you all for your continued support and allowing me to express my thoughts with you. It's greatly apprectiated!

SNEAK PEEK!

K.C. Mills Presents
It's Something About the Hood In Her
Nikki Brown

LET ME GO

"Cami trying my muthafuckin patience." Vinny said through clenched teeth as he watched her throw her ass on the man dancing behind her. The short skirt that she had on left nothing to the imagination and the way she was moving her body had Vinny heated. "She gone make me air this bitch out."

"Don't start no shit in here nigga." His sister Key walked up beside him and leaned over the rail, diverting her attention to what he was looking at. She could tell in his demeanor that he had seen something that he didn't like and more than likely it had to do with Cami seeing as though this was her night. "She asked you to slow down for her and you told her you couldn't. So, don't be mad when she pulls a you on you."

Vinny glared down at his sister; he was not in the mood to hear any of that. Cami knew what the deal with was when she decided to open her legs to him. They both were in the game and she knew what came along with being in the game. It wasn't his fault that she decided to switch things up, and he wasn't about to pick up the slack for her assumption that he was ready to hang up his hoe card.

Him and Cami had been dealing with each other for about a year and some change. In his heart, he knew that he wanted to be with her for the rest of his life, but he wasn't at a point in his life to accept it, at least not right now. His dick often contradicted what he felt in his heart and because he couldn't control that, he couldn't have Cami the way he wanted to.

Vinny knew he was a fuck up when it came to women, he couldn't help his impulsiveness with pussy. It was like when he was afforded the opportunity to move up in the Maler organization, the number of women after him increased and instead of thinking of Cami's feelings he gave into temptation often. He selfishly wanted Cami to be there waiting for him with open arms when he finally got it all out of his system but she wasn't having it.

Any man would be honored to have a woman like her on their team which is why he refused to see her happy with anyone else. He often took advantage of the fact that she loved him, what he didn't know was that she was almost at her breaking point.

"Yo Cas, come get Key aggravating ass before I throw her ugly ass over this banister." Vinny said over his shoulder to his sister's boyfriend. They had been rocking for a little minute. He loved Cassidy for Key and they got along great. He was about the only one that he knew that could put Key in her place.

"You can say whatever you want to say, but she has a right to live her life just like you have a right to live yours. You made your choice when you knocked up Jayla hoe ass." Key was over how her brother treated Cami and she had told her on more than one occasion that she should move on. Vinny was her brother, but she was a woman first and she didn't believe Cami deserved that.

Vinny bit down on his back teeth at the fact that Key brought up Jayla and her so called pregnancy. He knew just as well as anyone else that she wasn't pregnant, and if she was she didn't know for sure who the father was.

Vinny felt like it was a ploy for attention because he stopped fucking with her after she sent Cassidy a video of her playing with herself. She claimed it was by accident but Vinny didn't believe her. It wasn't like they were serious or anything like that, what they had was strictly physical but she wanted more, they all did.

"Bruh got damn you ain't gone help me out nigga?" he turned around and faced Cassidy who had a smirk on his face. Vinny shook his head and took that as a no. Turning back to the crowd, Vinny clenched his fist as he watched Cami grin in this nigga face like she didn't know he was there. "Fuck this."

Vinny waved Key off as he took off towards the stairs, everyone in their section held their breaths waiting for what he was going to do. He could be a loose cannon sometimes and it was hard to reel him back in when he got like that. Key just prayed that he didn't make a scene.

Vinny was Spiff's boy, his right-hand man, and he knew exactly what was about to happen. To keep the drama from unfolding, Spiff had already sent a text to his head of security to have the man removed from the club and for them not to let him past the ropes for VIP. He'd be pissed but Spiff couldn't afford the negative attention.

That was one of the only reasons that he hated that his right hand and his sister dealt with each other, he always felt like he was in the middle of it when he didn't want to be. He warned the both of them when it came out but neither took heed to his warnings. Now his worst nightmare was coming true.

Cami saw Vinny watching her but she didn't care, even though her heart was with him she was tired of being his fool. It was like he made it his business to hurt her and she hated it. If he wanted to play this little back and forth game, then she would too but she could guarantee that she could do it better.

She looked up to where he was standing and instead of meeting his menacing stare like before, she looked into the eyes of her brother who was shaking his head. Cami rolled her eyes and turned her attention back to the man that she was with at the bar.

"What has your attention beautiful?" The tall handsome man standing in front of her asked while looking down at her. She was easily the most beautiful woman in the place and he spotted her immediately, it was something about the way the short haircut framed her face and brought out the spark in her light brown eyes that drew him to her.

"Oh nothing, just looking around making sure everything is okay." Cami smiled coolly.

"Why, do you work here?" Mr. Handsome furrowed his brows while he awaited an answer from her.

"No I own it." Her tone wasn't cocky but it was full of confidence. The man's eyes stretched wide, he opened his mouth to say something right as two of her hired security guards walked her way. "What are you doing?" Cami exclaimed as Miller, the shorter of the guards grabbed the man who she had been spending time with since she walked on the dance floor.

When they didn't answer she looked up to where her family and friends were in the VIP. When Vinny's smile slowly spread across his face, she already knew what was up. Shaking her head, she followed behind the men that was dragging out her new friend.

"You work for me and if you don't stop right now, tomorrow will be spent at the unemployment office." Cami yelled getting heated. She was so tired of Vinny having so much control over her life she didn't know what to do. She had thoughts of leaving North Carolina and never looking back but her brother was here and the two were close.

"Sorry ma'am just following orders." Jao, the taller of the two answered.

"Vincent does not own this club!"

"No ma'am, Mr. Price had us escort him out. If you want him back in you will have to take that up with him." Jao stated confidently.

Cami's eyes traveled to the shinny Staci Adams loafers he had on all the way up to his deep-set eyes that held no emotion. Cami could tell that he was from the streets but so was she and if he kept it up she was gonna show him just how street she could get.

Before she could open her mouth to curse him out Spiff walked through the door that led to outside where they were. Her eyes narrowed in on him and he held up his hand to stop her from going off. He didn't want to hear it, their club couldn't run off emotions and he did what was best for their establishment.

Tonight was the grand opening of the night club that they decided to open. They needed a way to wash their money and they both decided to go in on a night club. It made sense. So the last thing that Spiff needed was for Vinny and Cami to mess that up with their bullshit.

He knew Vinny better than anyone and the look that he had in his eye was one that said he was about to set it off in the club and they didn't need to get shut down before they even got up and started up good.

"What the fuck Seth?" Cami yelled calling her brother by his government name.

"Camila you know how that nigga is." Spiff offered up a sympathetic look.

He tried to warn his sister when she first started sneaking

around with him. They thought he didn't know but he didn't get as far as he did with not knowing. He told her that Vinny was a special kind of crazy but she thought she knew better than he did and went through with it anyway. Now she was reaping what she had sewn.

"I'm grown as fuck and he don't tell me what to do. I don't know why y'all nigga's think the world has to stop because he pokes his chest out. I'll deflate that muthafucka real quick, I'm tired of his ass! We're not even together!" Cami yelled.

Her frustrations with the situation at hand were clear and she didn't know how much more of it that she could take. It didn't matter what she did or where she went, he was there. She couldn't shake Vinny if she tried, and she really tried.

"It don't matter if you grown, I told yo ass that nigga wasn't right in the head." Spiff shook his head, he knew that Vinny loved his sister but he also knew that he was young and dumb much like himself which is why he didn't judge them or their situation. As long as his sister was safe and unharmed, he didn't have shit to do with what they had going on no matter how much they tried to throw him in it. "If you would have kept on with your shit then that nigga would have shot up the fucking club, the fucking club that I put half on nigga. You really trying to have that shit crumble before it's actually fully built?"

"He ain't even old enough to be in that bitch anyway." Cami argued. Vinny was young, four years their junior, at 20 years old. "It's a 21 and up club that nigga shouldn't even been in there." Cami yelled pointing to the door and then she turned to see the gentlemen that she had just met. "I'm so sorry about this." She was embarrassed that he had heard the conversation with her and Spiff, for a minute she forgot that they were all still standing there. The security guards weren't sure what to do so they still had him jacked up right next to where the argument was taking place.

"But he's old enough to be in ya bed though." Spiff snarled his nose at her as he turned his attention to the man that was looking back and forth between the two of them. "What's ya name my man?" Spiff asked as he went into his pocket and pulled out a wad of money pulling two bills off the top and handing them to the man.

"Johnny." He said as he jerked away from the guards, the taller one chuckled at him trying to be bold now. "This is really unprofessional."

"I really don't give a fuck what you think is and isn't professional. None of that shit is my concern but I just wanted to pay you for your troubles and bid you a goodnight." Spiff slid his hands in his pockets and watched as Johnny gave Cami a disgusted look, then retreated to his car.

"This is some bullshit."

Cami spun on her heels and headed to the VIP section that she knew Vinny was in. When she got to the ropes, they were immediately opened for her. The short camel colored wrap skirt was rising up her thigh with every step that she took but she didn't care. She was tired of him dictating the things that she did and she vowed to put a stop to it.

When Vinny came into view, he was seated with one of

the many groupies that hung around him sitting on his lap. Cami strutted right over and grabbed the girl by her high ponytail and slung her to the ground. The girl jumped up immediately, but Vinny stopped her in her tracks.

"I dare you to touch her." Vinny didn't care what went on with him and Cami, he wasn't about to let anyone hurt her. Not that she needed anyone to protect her because she was as hood as it came and could probably shoot a gun better than him but it still wasn't going down in his presence.

"Oh now you care nigga?" Cami threw her hands up in the air letting them fall back down by her side, causing a slapping noise that could be heard over the music.

"Don't do that, you know I don't care about nothing but you." Vinny drug his tongue across his bottom lip and then delivered his award-winning smile.

Cami hated how her body responded to him, it was like when he was in her presence her body was in a trance and no longer taking orders from her brain. Her nipple's poked through the thin fabric of the camel colored, strapless top that graced her blemish free skin. The seat of her panties instantly became drenched when his eyes met hers.

She hated and wanted this man all at the same time, but she knew that they were no good for each other. She knew that, she just wished he would get on board. Cami was two seconds from going off on him when he pulled her down on his lap, shocking her.

"What are you doing Vincent?" she growled, calling him by his government name.

"Who the hell is Vincent?" the girl that previously held the spot on Vinny's lap asked.

She was a little pissed that Vinny had played her like that. She had met him on the block a little while ago and when she seen him in the club, she decided to shoot her shot. Everyone knew about Cami and the love he had for her but that didn't stop the women around him from trying to steal her spot in his heart, or the least in his bed.

"Yo why the fuck you still here?" Vinny peeked from behind Cami with a look of aggravation on his face.

"I thought we were chilling tonight." She whined.

"You thought wrong, scram."

"No she didn't, I'm not doing this with you Vincent. I'm too fucking old to be playing these little kid ass games with you. The back and forth shit is not my groove and I'm good on you." She tried to get up but he pulled her back down.

"We can do this the easy way or the hard way, I'll leave that up to you." He whispered in her ear causing her shoulders to shudder. He could feel her slipping away from him and he didn't know if he could take her leaving. So he was about to tell her what he thought she wanted to hear. "I'm done with all that bullshit."

Cami twisted up her lips and folded her arms across her chest. She didn't believe him no further than she could throw him and he wasn't a little nigga. She knew what he was doing and she wasn't about to let him do that.

"Vincent, why are we playing this game? You and I both know that you are dedicated to pussy and I get it, you're

young but don't hold me back because you want to be selfish."
Cami softened her tone and stared deeply into his eyes. She
wanted to him to listen to the words that left her lips and not
just agree to something so she would be quiet, like he
normally did. "If you love me like you say you did you
wouldn't hold me back from being happy." She touched his
face softly.

Vinny slapped her hand away from him and grilled her
causing her to roll her eyes in the back of her head. He
couldn't believe that she was trying to be all sweet to him
while pretty much telling him that she didn't want to deal
with him anymore.

"You trying to finesse a nigga?" He tilted his head. "I love
you so I can't let you go. I can't explain that shit Cami. It's
like the thought of you walking out of my life takes my breath
away, like on some hoe shit. Real nigga shit I get hives and
start itching at the thought of you not fucking with me no
more. I can't handle that shit." Vinny touched his heart and
blinked a few times.

Cami just looked at him disgustedly, "See that's your
fucking problem you think everything is a fucking joke
Vinny." She yelled hopping off of his lap. "Just leave me the
hell alone. I'm done with this shit." She stomped out of the
section and Vinny finally released a smile.

"Nigga the fuck you just do that for?" Spiff stood in front
of him.

"Man shut the fuck up and duck nigga, wifey headed up
the steps." Vinny laughed and Spiff turned around to watch

the mother of his one year old son strut up the stairs like she owned the place.

"This about to be a long fucking night." Spiff huffed as he snatched the bottle of Henny off of the table and went to find his twin.

Coming Soon!!!

CPSIA information can be obtained
at www.ICGtesting.com
Printed in the USA
LVHW110829190719
624531LV00011B/457/P